Harry Harrison was born in Stamford,
Connecticut, in 1925 and lived in New York
City until 1943, when he joined the United
States Army. He was a machine-gun instructor
during the war, but returned to his art studies
after leaving the army.

Apart from enjoying an enviable reputation as
one of the best writers on the science fiction
scene, Harry Harrison is a well travelled man
of wide interests and accomplishments. A first-
class short story writer, an experienced editor
and anthologist, a translator, a trained
cartoonist, he has also been a commercial
illustrator, an art director, an hydraulic press
operator, a truck driver, and is, of course, a
first-rate novelist.

Harrison's style leaps from the humour of his
Stainless Steel Rat novels, to purist sf, to
splendid combinations of fantasy and science
fiction.

Also by Harry Harrison in Sphere Books:

DEATHWORLD 2
DEATHWORLD 3
THE STAINLESS STEEL RAT
THE STAINLESS STEEL RAT'S REVENGE
THE STAINLESS STEEL RAT SAVES THE WORLD
THE STAINLESS STEEL RAT WANTS YOU
THE STAINLESS STEEL RAT FOR PRESIDENT
PLAGUE FROM SPACE
TWO TALES AND EIGHT TOMORROWS
PRIME NUMBER
INVASION: EARTH
PLANET OF NO RETURN

Deathworld 1

HARRY HARRISON

SPHERE SCIENCE FICTION AND FANTASY
LIBRARY

SPHERE BOOKS LIMITED
London and Sydney

First published in Great Britain in 1963
by Penguin Books Ltd
Copyright © Harry Harrison 1960
Published by Sphere Books 1973
30–32 Gray's Inn Road, London WC1X 8JL
Reprinted 1974, 1977, 1979, 1980, 1982, 1983, 1984, 1985

For Joan

TRADE
MARK

Set in Intertype Plantin

Printed in Great Britain by
Hazell Watson & Viney Limited,
Aylesbury, Bucks

CHAPTER ONE

With a gentle sigh the service tube dropped a message capsule into the receiving cup. The attention bell chimed once and was silent. Jason dinAlt stared at the harmless capsule as though it were a ticking bomb.

Something was going wrong. He felt a hard knot of tension form inside of him. This was no routine service memo or hotel communication, but a sealed personal message. Yet he knew no one on this planet, having arrived by spacer less than eight hours earlier. Since even his name was new – dating back to the last time he had changed ships – there could be no personal messages. Yet here one was.

Stripping the seal with his thumbnail, he took the top off. The recorder in the pencil-sized capsule gave the taped voice a tinny sound with no clues as to the speaker.

'Kerk Pyrrus would like to see Jason dinAlt. I'm waiting in the lobby.'

It was wrong, yet it couldn't be avoided. Chances were that the man was harmless. A salesman perhaps or a case of mistaken identity. Nevertheless Jason carefully positioned his gun behind a pillow on the couch, with the safety off. There was no way to predict how these things would turn out. He signalled the desk to send the visitor up. When the door opened, Jason was slumped down on a corner of the couch, sipping from a tall glass.

A retired wrestler. That was Jason's first thought when the man came through the door. Kerk Pyrrus was a grey-haired rock of a man, his body apparently chiselled out of flat slabs of muscle. His grey clothes were so conservative they were almost a uniform. Strapped to his forearm was a rugged and much-worn holster, a gun-muzzle peering blankly from it.

'You're dinAlt the gambler,' the stranger said bluntly. 'I have a proposition for you.'

Jason looked across the top of his glass, letting his mind play with the probabilities. This was either the police or the com-

5

petition – and he wanted nothing to do with either. He had to know a lot more before he became involved in any deals.

'Sorry, friend,' Jason smiled, 'But you have the wrong party. Like to oblige, but my gambling always seems to help the casinos more than myself. So you see . . .'

'Let's not play games with each other,' Kerk broke in with a chesty rumble. 'You're dinAlt and you're Bohel as well. If you want more names, I'll mention Mahaut's Planet, the Nebula Casino and plenty more. I have a proposition that will benefit both of us, and you had better listen to it.'

None of the names caused the slightest change in Jason's half-smile. But his body was tensely alert. This musclebound stranger knew things he had no right to know. It was time to change the subject.

'That's quite a gun you have there,' Jason said. 'But guns make me nervous. I'd appreciate it if you took it off.'

Kerk scowled down at the gun, as if he were seeing it for the first time. 'No, I never take it off.' He seemed mildly annoyed by the suggestion.

The testing period was over. Jason needed the upper hand if he was to get out of this one alive. As he leaned forward to put his drink on the table, his other hand fell naturally behind the pillow. He was touching the gun-butt when he said, 'I'm afraid I'll have to insist. I always feel a little uncomfortable around people who are armed.' He kept talking to distract attention while he pulled out his gun. Fast and smooth.

He could have been moving in slow motion for all the difference it made. Kerk Pyrrus stood dead still while the gun came out, while it swung in his direction. Not until the very last instant did he act. When he did, the motion wasn't visible. First his gun was in the arm-holster – then it was aimed between Jason's eyes. It was an ugly, heavy weapon with a pitted front orifice that showed plenty of use.

Jason knew if he swung his own weapon up a fraction of an inch more he would be dead. He dropped his arm carefully, angry at himself for trying to substitute violence for thought. Kerk flipped his own gun back into the holster with the same ease he had drawn it.

'Enough of that now,' Kerk said. 'Let's get down to business.'

Jason reached out and downed a large mouthful from his glass, bridling his temper. He was fast with a gun – his life had depended on it more than once – and this was the first time he had ever been outdrawn. It was the off-hand, unimportant manner it had been done that irritated him.

'I'm not prepared to do business,' he said acidly. 'I've come to Cassylia for a vacation, get away from work.'

'Let's not fool each other, dinAlt,' Kerk said impatiently. 'You've never worked at an honest job in your entire life. You're a professional gambler and that's why I'm here to see you.'

Jason forced down his anger and threw the gun to the other end of the couch so he wouldn't be tempted to commit suicide. He had been so sure that no one knew him on Cassylia and had been looking forward to a big kill at the Casino. He would worry about that later. This wrestler type seemed to know all the answers. Let him plot the course for a while and see where it led.

'All right, what do you want?'

Kerk dropped into a chair that creaked ominously under his weight, and dug an envelope out of one pocket. He flipped through it quickly and dropped a handful of gleaming Galactic Exchange Notes on to the table. Jason glanced at them – then sat up suddenly.

'What are they – forgeries?' he asked, holding one up to the light.

'They're real enough,' Kerk told him, 'I picked them up at the bank. Exactly twenty-seven bills – or twenty-seven million credits. I want you to use them as a bankroll when you go to the Casino tonight. Gamble with them and win.'

They looked real enough – and they could be checked. Jason fingered them thoughtfully while he examined the other man.

'I don't know what you have in mind,' he said. 'But you realize I can't make any guarantees. I gamble – but I don't always win.'

'You gamble – and you win when you want to,' Kerk said grimly. 'We looked into that quite carefully before I came to you.'

'If you mean to say that I cheat . . .' Carefully, Jason grabbed

7

his temper again and held it down. There was no future in getting annoyed.

Kerk continued in the same level voice, ignoring Jason's growing anger: 'Maybe you don't call it cheating, frankly I don't care. As far as I'm concerned, you could have your sleeves lined with aces and electromagnets in your toes. As long as you win. I'm not here to discuss moral points with you. I said I had a proposition.

'We have worked hard for that money – but it still isn't enough. To be precise, we need three thousand million credits. The only way to get that sum is by gambling. With these twenty-seven million as bankroll.'

'And what do I get out of it?' Jason asked the question coolly, as if any bit of the fantastic proposition made sense.

'Everything above three thousand million you can keep, that should be fair enough. You're not risking your own money, but you stand to make enough to keep you for life if you win.'

'And if I lose?'

Kerk thought for a moment, not liking the taste of the idea. 'Yes, there is the chance you might lose. I hadn't thought about that.'

He reached a decision. 'If you lose – well, I suppose that is just a risk we will have to take. Though I think I would kill you then. The ones who died to get the twenty-seven million deserve at least that.' He said it quietly, without malice, and it was more of a considered decision than a threat.

Stamping to his feet, Jason refilled his glass and offered one to Kerk who took it with a nod of thanks. He paced back and forth, unable to sit. The whole proposition made him angry, yet at the same time had a fatal fascination. He was a gambler and this talk was like the sight of drugs to an addict.

Stopping suddenly, he realized that his mind had been made up for some time. Win or lose – live or die – how could he say no to the chance to gamble with money like that! He turned suddenly and jabbed his finger at the big man in the chair.

'I'll do it – you probably knew I would from the time you came in here. There are some terms of my own, though. I want to know who you are, and who *they* are you keep talking about.

8

And where did the money come from – is it stolen?'

Kerk drained his own glass and pushed it away from him.

'Stolen money? No, quite the opposite. Two years' work mining and refining ore to get it. It was mined on Pyrrus and sold here on Cassylia. You can check on that very easily. I sold it. I'm the Pyrric ambassador to this planet.' He smiled at the thought. 'Not that that means much. I'm ambassador to at least six other planets as well. Comes in handy when you want to do business.'

Jason looked at the muscular man with his grey hair and worn, military-cut clothes, and decided not to laugh. You heard of strange things out in the frontier planets and every word could be true. He had never heard of Pyrrus either, though that didn't mean anything. There were over thirty thousand known planets in the inhabited universe.

'I'll check on what you have told me,' Jason said. 'If it's true we can do business. Call me tomorrow. . . .'

'No,' Kerk said. 'The money has to be won tonight. I've already issued a cheque for this twenty-seven million; it will bounce as high as the Pleiades unless we deposit the money in the morning, so that's our time limit.'

With each moment, the whole affair became more fantastic – and more intriguing for Jason. He looked at his watch. There was still enough time to find out if Kerk was lying or not.

'All right, we'll do it tonight,' he said. 'Only I'll have to have one of those bills to verify.'

Kerk stood up to go. 'Take them all, I won't be seeing you again until after you've won. I'll be at the Casino, of course, but don't recognize me. It would be much better if they didn't know where your money was coming from or how much you had.'

Then he was gone, after a bone-crushing handclasp that closed on Jason's hand like vice-jaws. Jason was alone with the money. Fanning the bills out like a hand of cards, he stared at their sepia-and-gold faces, trying to get the reality through his head. Twenty-seven million credits. What was to stop him from just walking out the door with them and vanishing? Nothing really, except his own sense of honour.

Kerk Pyrrus, the man with the same last name as the planet he came from, was the universe's biggest fool. Or he knew just

9

what he was doing. From the way the interview had gone, the latter seemed the best bet.

'He *knows* I would much rather gamble with the money than steal it,' he said wryly.

Slipping a small gun into his waistband holster and pocketing the money, he went out.

CHAPTER TWO

The robot teller at the bank just pinged with electronic shock when he presented one of the bills and flashed a panel that directed him to see Vice-President Wain. Wain was a smooth customer who bugged his eyes and lost some of his tan when he saw the sheaf of bills.

'You – wish to deposit these with us?' he asked while his fingers unconsciously stroked them.

'Not today,' Jason said. 'They were paid to me as a debt. Would you please check that they are authentic and change them. I'd like five hundred thousand credit notes.'

Both of his inner chest pockets were packed tight when he left the bank. The bills were good and he felt like a walking mint. This was the first time in his entire life that carrying a large sum of money made him uncomfortable. Waving to a passing helicab, he went directly to the Casino where he knew he would be safe. For a while.

Cassylia Casino was the playspot of the near-by cluster of star systems. It was the first time Jason had seen it, though he knew its type well. He had spent most of his adult life in casinos like this on other worlds. The *décor* differed but they were always the same. Gambling and socialities in public – and behind the scenes all the private vice you could afford. Theoretically no-limit games, but that was true only up to a certain point. When the house was really hurt, the honest games stopped being square and the big winner had to watch his step very carefully. These were the odds Jason dinAlt had played against countless times before. He was wary but not very concerned.

The dining-room was almost empty and the majordomo quickly rushed to the side of the stranger in the richly cut clothes. Jason was lean and dark and moved with a positive, self-assured manner. More like the owner of inherited wealth than a professional gambler. This appearance was important and he cultivated it. The cuisine looked good and the cellar turned out to be wonderful. He had a professional and enthusiastic talk with the wine steward while waiting for the soup, then settled down to enjoy his meal.

He ate leisurely and the large dining-room was filled before he was through. Watching the entertainment over a long cigar killed some more time. When he finally went to the gaming-rooms, they were filled and active.

Moving slowly around the room, he dropped a few thousand credits. He scarcely noticed how he played, giving more attention to the feel of the games. The play all seemed honest and none of the equipment was rigged. That could be changed very quickly, he realized. Usually it wasn't necessary; house percentage was enough to assure a profit.

Once he saw Kerk out of the corner of his eye, but he paid him no attention. The ambassador was losing small sums steadily at seven-and-silver and seemed to be impatient. Probably waiting for Jason to begin playing seriously. He smiled and strolled on slowly.

Jason settled on the dice table as he usually did. It was the surest way to make small winnings. *And if I feel it tonight, I can clean this casino out!* That was his secret, the power that won for him steadily – and every once in a while enabled him to make a killing and move on quickly before the hired thugs came to get the money back.

The dice reached him and he threw an eight the hard way. Betting was light and he didn't push himself, just kept away from the sevens. He made the point and passed a natural. Then he crapped out and the dice moved on.

Sitting there, making small automatic bets while the dice went around the table, he thought about the power. *Funny, after all the years of work, we still don't know much about* psi. *They can train people a bit, and improve skills a bit – but that's all.*

He was feeling strong tonight, he knew that the money in his pocket gave him the extra lift that sometimes helped him break through. With his eyes half closed he picked up the dice – and let his mind gently caress the pattern of sunken dots. Then they shot out of his hand and he stared at a seven.

It was there.

Stronger than he had felt it in years. The stiff weight of the million credits had done it. The world all around was sharp-cut and clear and the dice were completely in his control. He knew to the tenth credit how much the other players had in their wallets and was aware of the cards in the hands of the players behind him.

Slowly, carefully, he built up the stakes.

There was no effort to the dice; they rolled and sat up like trained dogs. Jason took his time and concentrated on the psychology of the players and the stickman. It took almost two hours to build his money on the table to seven hundred thousand credits. Then he caught the stickman signalling they had a heavy winner. He waited until the hard-eyed man strolled over to watch the game, then he breathed on the dice, bet all his table stakes – and blew it all with a single roll. The houseman smiled happily, the stickman relaxed – and, out of the corner of his eye, Jason saw Kerk turning a dark purple.

Sweating, pale, his hands trembling ever so slightly, Jason opened the front of his jacket and pulled out one of the envelopes of new bills. Breaking the seal with his finger, he dropped two of them on the table.

'Could we have a no-limit game?' he asked. 'I'd like to – win back some of my money.'

The stickman had trouble controlling his smile now, he glanced across at the houseman who nodded a quick *yes*. They had a sucker and they meant to clean him. He had been playing from his wallet all evening; now he was cracking into a sealed envelope to try for what he had lost. A thick envelope, too, and probably not his money. Not that the house cared in the least. To them money had no loyalties. The play went on with the Casino in a very relaxed mood.

Which was just the way Jason wanted it. He needed to get as deep into them as he could before someone realized *they* might be on the losing end. The rough stuff would start and he wanted to put it off as long as possible. It would be hard to win smoothly – and his *psi* power might go as quickly as it had come. That had happened before.

He was playing against the house now, the two other players were obvious shills, and a crowd had jammed solidly around to watch. After losing and winning a bit, he hit a streak of naturals and his pile of gold chips tottered higher and higher. There was nearly a thousand million there, he estimated roughly. The dice were still falling true, though he was soaked with sweat from the effort. Betting the entire stack of chips, he reached for the dice. The stickman reached faster and hooked them away.

'House calls for new dice,' he said flatly.

Jason straightened up and wiped his hands, glad of the instant's relief. This was the third time the house had changed dice to try and break his winning streak. It was their privilege. The hard-eyed Casino man opened his wallet as he had done before and drew out a pair at random. Stripping off their plastic cover, he threw them the length of the table to Jason. They came up a natural seven and Jason smiled.

When he scooped them up, the smile slowly faded. The dice were transparent, finely made, evenly weighted on all sides – and crooked.

The pigment on the dots of five sides of each dice was some heavy metal compound, probably lead. The sixth side was a ferric compound. They would roll true unless they hit a magnetic field – which meant the entire surface of the table could be magnetized. He could never have spotted the difference if he hadn't *looked* at the dice with his mind. But what could he do about it?

Shaking them slowly, he glanced quickly around the table. There was what he needed. An ashtray with a magnet in its base to hold it to the metal edge of the table. Jason stopped shaking the dice and looked at them quizzically, then reached over and grabbed the ashtray. He dropped the base against his hand.

As he lifted the ashtray, there was a concerted gasp from

all sides. The dice were sticking there, upside-down, boxcars showing.

'Are these what you call honest dice?' he asked.

The man who had thrown out the dice reached quickly for his hip pocket. Jason was the only one who saw what happened next. He was watching that hand closely, his own fingers near his gun-butt. As the man dived into his pocket, a hand reached out of the crowd behind him. From its square-cut size, it could have belonged to only one person. The thick thumb and index finger clamped swiftly around the houseman's wrist, then they were gone. The man screamed shrilly and held up his arm, his hand dangling limp as a glove from the broken wrist bones.

With his flank well protected, Jason could go on with the game. 'The old dice, if you don't mind,' he said quietly.

Dazedly the stickman pushed them over. Jason shook quickly and rolled. Before they hit the table, he realized he couldn't control them – the transient *psi* power had gone.

End over end they turned. And faced up seven.

Counting the chips as they were pushed over to him, he added up a bit under a thousand million credits. They would be winning that much if he left the game now – but it wasn't the three thousand million that Kerk needed. Well, it would have to be enough. As he reached for the chips he caught Kerk's eye across the table and the other man shook his head in a steady *no*.

'Let it ride,' Jason said wearily, 'one more roll.'

He breathed on the dice, polished them on his cuff, and wondered how he had ever gotten into this spot. Thousands of millions riding on a pair of dice. That was as much as the annual income of some planets. The only thing that made it possible to have stakes like that was the fact that the planetary government had a controlling interest in the Casino. He shook as long as he could, reaching for the control that wasn't there – then let fly.

Everything else had stopped in the Casino and people were standing on tables and chairs to watch. There wasn't a sound from that large crowd. The dice bounced back from the board with a clatter loud in the silence and tumbled over the cloth.

A five and a one. Six. He still had to make his point. Scooping up the dice, Jason talked to them, mumbled the ancient oaths that brought luck and threw again.

It took five throws before he made the six.

The crowd echoed his sigh and their voices rose quickly. He wanted to stop, take a deep breath, but he knew he couldn't. Winning the money was only part of the job – they now had to get away with it. It had to look casual. A waiter was passing with a tray of drinks. Jason stopped him and tucked a one hundred credit note in his pocket.

'Drinks are on me,' he shouted while he pried the tray out of the waiter's hands. Well-wishers cleared the filled glasses away quickly and Jason piled the chips on to the tray. They more than loaded it, but Kerk appeared that moment with a second tray.

'I'll be glad to help you, sir, if you will permit me,' he said.

Jason looked at him and laughed permission. It was the first time he had a clear look at Kerk in the Casino. He was wearing loose, purple evening pyjamas over what must have been a false stomach. The sleeves were long and baggy, so he looked fat rather than muscular. It was a simple but effective disguise.

Carefully carrying the loaded trays, surrounded by a crowd of excited patrons, they made their way to the cashier's window. The manager himself was there, wearing a forced grin. Even the grin faded when he counted the chips.

'Could you come back in the morning,' he said. 'I'm afraid we don't have that kind of money on hand.'

'What's the matter,' Kerk shouted, 'trying to get out of paying him? You took *my* money easy enough when I lost – it works both ways!'

The onlookers, always happy to see the house lose, growled their disagreement. Jason finished the matter in a loud voice.

'I'll be reasonable. Give me what cash you have and I'll take a cheque for the balance.'

There was no way out. Under the watchful eye of the gleeful crowd, the manager packed an envelope with bills and wrote a cheque. Jason took a quick glimpse at it, then stuffed it into an inside pocket. With the envelope under one arm, he followed Kerk towards the door.

Because of the onlookers, there was no trouble in the main

room, but just as they reached the side entrance two men moved in, blocking their way.

'Just a moment,' one said. He never finished the sentence. Kerk walked into them without slowing and they bounced away like tenpins. Then Kerk and Jason were out of the building and walking fast.

'Into the parking lot,' Kerk said. 'I have a car there.'

When they rounded the corner, there was a car bearing down on them. Before Jason could get his gun clear of the holster, Kerk was in front of him. His arm came up and his big ugly gun burst through the cloth of his sleeve and jumped into his hand. A single shot killed the driver and the car swerved and crashed. The other two men in the car died coming out of the door, their guns dropping from their hands.

After that they had no trouble. Kerk drove at top speed away from the Casino, the torn sleeve of his pyjamas whipping in the breeze, giving glimpses of the big gun back in the holster.

'When you get the chance,' Jason said, 'you'll have to show me how that trick holster works.'

'When we get the chance,' Kerk answered as he dived the car into the city access tube.

CHAPTER THREE

The building they stopped at was one of the finer residences in Cassylia. As they had driven, Jason counted the money and separated his share. Almost sixteen million credits. It still didn't seem quite real. When they got out in front of the building, he gave Kerk the rest.

'Here's your three thousand million. Don't think it was easy,' he said.

'It could have been worse,' was his only answer.

The recorded voice scratched in the speaker over the door. 'Sire Ellus has retired for the night, would you please call again in the morning. All appointments are made in advance—'

The voice broke off as Kerk pushed the door open. He did it

almost effortlessly with the flat of his hand. As they went in, Jason looked at the remnants of torn and twisted metal that hung in the lock and wondered again about his companion.

Strength – more than physical strength – he's like an elemental force. I have the feeling that nothing can stop him.

It made him angry – and at the same time fascinated him. He didn't want out of the deal until he found out more about Kerk and his planet. And 'they' who had died for the money he gambled.

Sire Ellus was old, balding and angry, not at all used to having his rest disturbed. His companions stopped suddenly when Kerk threw the money down on the table.

'Is the ship being loaded yet, Ellus? Here's the balance due.' Ellus only fumbled the bills for a moment before he could answer Kerk's question.

'The ship – but of course. We began loading when you gave us the deposit. You'll have to excuse my confusion; this is a little irregular. We never handle transactions of this size in cash.'

'That's the way I like to do business,' Kerk answered him. 'I've cancelled the deposit, this is the total sum. Now how about a receipt?'

Ellus had made out the receipt before his senses returned. He held it tightly while he looked uncomfortably at the three thousand millions spread out before him.

'Wait – I can't take it now, you'll have to return in the morning, to the bank. In normal business fashion,' Ellus decided firmly.

Kerk reached over and gently drew the paper out of Ellus's hand.

'Thanks for the receipt,' he said. 'I won't be here in the morning so this will be satisfactory. And if you're worried about the money, I suggest you get in touch with most of your plant guards or private police. You'll feel a lot safer.'

When they left through the shattered door, Ellus was frantically dialling numbers on his screen. Kerk answered Jason's next question before he could ask it.

'I imagine you would like to live to spend that money in your pocket, so I've booked us two seats on an interplanetary ship.' He glanced at the car clock. 'It leaves in about two hours so we have plenty of time. I'm hungry, let's find a restaurant. I hope you have nothing at the hotel worth going back for. It would be a little difficult.'

'Nothing worth getting killed for,' Jason said. 'Now where can we go to eat? There are a few questions I would like to ask you.'

They circled carefully down to the transport levels until they were sure they hadn't been followed. Kerk nosed the car into a shadowed loading dock where they abandoned it.

'We can always get another car,' he said, 'and they probably have this one spotted. Let's walk back to the freightway, I saw a restaurant there as we came by.'

Dark and looming shapes of overland freight carriers filled the parking lot. They picked their way around the man-high wheels and into the hot and noisy restaurant. The drivers and early morning workers took no notice of them as they found a booth in the back and dialled a meal.

Kerk chiselled a chunk of meat off the slab in front of him and popped it cheerfully into his mouth. 'Ask your questions,' he said. 'I'm feeling much better already.'

'What's in this ship you arranged for tonight? What kind of a cargo was I risking my neck for?'

'I thought you were risking your neck for money,' Kerk said dryly. 'But be assured it was in a good cause. That cargo means the survival of a world. Guns, ammunition, mines, explosives and such.'

Jason choked over a mouthful of food. 'Gun-running! What are you doing, financing a private war? And how can you talk about survival with a lethal cargo like that? Don't try and tell me they have a peaceful use. Who are you killing?'

Most of the big man's humour had vanished: he had that grim look Jason knew well.

'Yes, peaceful would be the right word. Because that is basically all we want. Just to live in peace. And it is not *who* are we killing – it is *what* we are killing.'

Jason pushed his plate away with an angry gesture. 'You're talking in riddles,' he said. 'What you say has no meaning.'

'It has meaning enough,' Kerk told him. 'But only on one

planet in the universe. Just how much do you know about Pyrrus?'

'Absolutely nothing.'

For a moment Kerk sat wrapped in memory, scowling distantly. Then he went on.

'Mankind doesn't belong on Pyrrus – yet has been there for almost three hundred years now. The age expectancy of my people is sixteen years. Of course most adults live beyond that, but the high child mortality brings the average down.

'It is everything that a humanoid world should not be. The gravity is nearly twice earth normal. The temperature can vary daily from arctic to tropic. The climate – well, you have to experience it to believe it. Like nothing you've seen anywhere else in the galaxy.'

'I'm frightened,' Jason said dryly. 'What do you have, methane or chlorine reactions? I've been down on planets like that –'

Kerk slammed his hand down hard on the table. The dishes bounced and the table-legs creaked. 'Laboratory reactions!' he growled. 'They look great on a bench – but what happens when you have a world filled with those compounds? In an eye-wink of galactic time all the violence is locked up in nice, stable compounds. The atmosphere may be poisonous for an oxygen breather, but taken by itself it's as harmless as weak beer.

'There is only one set-up that is pure poison as a planetary atmosphere. Plenty of H_2O, the most universal solvent you can find, plus free oxygen to work on –'

'Water and oxygen!' Jason broke in. 'You mean Earth – or a planet like Cassylia here? That's preposterous.'

'Not at all. Because you were born in this kind of environment, you accept it as right and natural. You take it for granted that metals corrode, coastlines change, and storms interfere with communications. These are normal occurrences on oxygen-water worlds. On Pyrrus these conditions are carried to the nth degree.

'The planet has an axial tilt of almost 42°, so there is a tremendous range of temperature from season to season. This is one of the prime causes of a constantly changing icecap. The weather generated by this is spectacular to say the least.'

'If that's all,' Jason said, 'I don't see why . . .'

'That's *not* all — it's barely the beginning. The open seas perform the dual destructive function of supplying water vapour to keep the weather going, and building up gigantic tides. Pyrrus's two satellites, Samas and Bessos, combine at times to pull the oceans up into thirty metre tides. And until you've seen one of these tides lap over into an active volcano you've seen nothing.

'Heavy elements are what brought us to Pyrrus — and these same elements keep the planet at a volcanic boil. There have been at least thirteen supernovas in the immediate stellar neighbourhood. Heavy elements can be found on most of their planets of course — as well as completely unbreathable atmospheres. Long-term mining and exploitation can't be done by anything but a self-sustaining colony. Which meant Pyrrus, where the radioactive elements are locked in the planetary core, surrounded by a shell of lighter ones. While this allows for the atmosphere men need, it also provides unceasing volcanic activity as the molten plasma forces its way to the surface.'

For the first time, Jason was silent. Trying to imagine what life could be like on a planet constantly at war with itself.

'I've saved the best for last,' Kerk said with grim humour. 'Now that you have an idea of what the environment is like — think of the kind of life forms that would populate it. I doubt if there is one off-world species that would live a minute. Plants and animals on Pyrrus are *tough*. They fight the world and they fight each other. Hundreds of thousands of years of genetic weeding-out have produced things that would give even an electronic brain nightmares. Armour-plated, poisonous, claw-tipped and fang-mouthed. That describes everything that walks, flaps or just sits and grows. Ever seen a plant with teeth — that bite? I don't think you want to. You'd have to be on Pyrrus and that means you would be dead within seconds of leaving the ship. Even I'll have to take a refresher course before I'll be able to go outside the landing buildings. The unending war for survival keeps the life forms competing and changing. Death is simple, but the ways of dealing it too numerous to list.'

Unhappiness rose like a weight on Kerk's broad shoulders. After long moments of thought, he moved visibly to shake it off. Returning his attention to his food and mopping the gravy from his plate, he voiced part of his feelings.

'I suppose there is no logical reason why we should stay and fight this endless war. Except that Pyrrus is our home.' The last piece of gravy-soaked bread vanished and he waved the empty fork at Jason.

'Be happy you're an off-worlder and will never have to see it.'

'That's where you're wrong,' Jason said as calmly as he could. 'You see, I'm going back with you.'

CHAPTER FOUR

'Don't talk stupidly,' Kerk said as he punched for a duplicate order of steak. 'There are much simpler ways of committing suicide. Don't you realize that you're a millionaire now? With what you have in your pocket, you can relax the rest of your life on the pleasure planets. Pyrrus is a death world, not a sight-seeing spot for jaded tourists. I cannot permit you to return with me.'

Gamblers who lose their tempers don't last long. Jason was angry now. Yet it showed only in a negative way, in the lack of expression on his face and the calmness of his voice.

'Don't tell me what I can or cannot do, Kerk Pyrrus. You're a big man with a fast gun – but that doesn't make you my keeper. All you can do is stop me from going back on your ship. But I can easily afford to get there another way. And don't try to tell me I want to go to Pyrrus for sightseeing when you have no idea of my real reasons.'

Jason didn't even try to explain his reasons, they were only half realized and too personal. The more he travelled, the more things looked the same to him. The old, civilized planets sank into a drab similarity. Frontier worlds all had the crude sameness of temporary camps in a forest. Not that the galactic worlds bored him. It was just that he had found their limitations – yet had never found his own. Until he met Kerk he had acknowledged no man his superior, or even his equal. This was more than egotism. It was facing facts. Now he was forced to face the fact that there was a whole world of people who might be superior to him. Jason could never rest content until he had been there and seen for himself. Even if he died in the attempt.

None of this could be told to Kerk. There were other reasons he would understand better.

'You're not thinking ahead when you prevent me from going to Pyrrus,' Jason said. 'I'll not mention any moral debt you owe me for winning that money you needed. But what about the next time? If you needed that much lethal goods once, you'll probably need it again some day. Wouldn't it be better to have me on hand – old tried and true – than dreaming up some new and possibly unreliable scheme?'

Kerk chewed pensively on the second serving of steak. 'That makes sense. And I must admit I hadn't thought of it before. One failing we Pyrrans have is a lack of interest in the future. Staying alive day by day is enough trouble. So we tend to face emergencies as they arrive and let the dim future take care of itself. You can come. I hope you will still be alive when we need you. As Pyrran ambassador to a lot of places I officially invite you to our planet. All expenses paid. On the condition you obey completely all our instructions regarding your personal safety.'

'Condition accepted,' Jason said. And wondered why he was so cheerful about signing his own death warrant.

Kerk was shovelling his way through his third dessert when his alarm watch gave a tiny hum. He dropped his fork instantly and stood up. 'Time to go,' he said. 'We're on schedule now.' While Jason scrambled to his feet, he jammed coins into the meter until the *paid* light came on. Then they were out the door and walking fast.

Jason wasn't at all surprised when they came on a public escalator just behind the restaurant. He was beginning to realize that since leaving the Casino their every move had been carefully planned and timed. Without a doubt, the alarm was out and the entire planet being searched for them. Yet so far they hadn't noticed the slightest sign of pursuit. This wasn't the first time Jason had to move just one jump ahead of the authorities – but it was the first time he had let someone else lead him by the hand while he did it. He had to smile at his own automatic agreement. He had been a loner for so many years that he found a certain inverse pleasure in following someone else.

'Hurry up,' Kerk growled after a quick glance at his watch. He set a steady, killing pace up the escalator steps. They went up five levels that way – without seeing another person – before Kerk relented and let the escalator do the work.

Jason prided himself on keeping in condition. But the sudden climb, after the sleepless night, left him panting heavily and soaked with sweat. Kerk, cool of forehead and breathing normally, didn't show the slightest sign that he had been running.

They were at the second motor level when Kerk stepped off the slowly rising steps and waved Jason after him. As they came through the exit to the street a car pulled up to the kerb in front of them. Jason had enough sense not to reach for his gun. At the exact moment they reached the car, the driver opened the door and stepped out. Kerk passed him a slip of paper without saying a word and slipped in behind the wheel. There was just time for Jason to jump in before the car pulled away. The entire transfer had taken less than three seconds.

There had only been a glimpse of the driver in the dim light, but Jason had recognized him. Of course he had never seen the man before, but after knowing Kerk he couldn't mistake the compact strength of a native Pyrran.

'That was the receipt from Ellus you gave him,' Jason said.

'Of course. That takes care of the ship and the cargo. They'll be off-planet and safely away before the Casino cheque is traced to Ellus. So now let's look after ourselves. I'll explain the plan in detail so there will be no slip-ups on your part. I'll go through the whole thing once and if there are any questions you'll ask them only when I'm finished.'

The tones of command were so automatic that Jason found

himself listening in quiet obedience. Though one part of his mind wanted him to smile at the quick assumption of his incompetence.

Kerk swung the car into the steady line of traffic heading out of the city to the spaceport. He drove easily while he talked.

'There is a search on in the city, but we're well ahead of that. I'm sure the Cassylians don't want to advertise their bad sportsmanship, so there won't be anything as crude as a roadblock. But the port will be crawling with every agent they have. They know once the money gets off-planet, it is gone for ever. When we make a break for it they will be sure we still have the cash. So there will be no trouble with the munition ship getting clear.'

Jason sounded a little shocked. 'You mean you're setting us up as clay pigeons to cover the take-off of the ship.'

'You could put it that way. But since we have to get off-planet anyway, there is no harm in using our escape as a smoke-screen. Now shut up until I've finished, like I told you. One more interruption and I dump you by the road.'

Jason was sure he would. He listened intently – and quietly – as Kerk repeated word for word what he had said before, then continued:

'The official car gate will probably be wide open with the traffic through it. And a lot of agents will be in plain clothes. We might even get on to the field without being recognized, thought I doubt it. It is of no importance. We will drive through the gate and to the take-off pad. The *Pride of Darkhan*, for which we hold tickets, will be sounding its two-minute siren and unhooking the gangway. By the time we get to our seats, the ship will take off.'

'That's all very fine,' Jason said. 'But what will the guards be doing all this time?'

'Shooting at us and each other. We will take advantage of the confusion to get aboard.'

This answer did nothing to settle Jason's mind, but he let it slide for the moment. 'All right, say we *do* get aboard. Why don't they just prevent take-off until we have been dragged out and stood against a wall?'

Kerk spared him a contemptuous glance before he returned

24

his eyes to the road. 'I said the ship was the *Pride of Darkhan*. If you had studied this system at all, you would know what that means. Cassylia and Darkhan are sister planets and rivals in every way. It has been less than two centuries since they fought an intra-system war that almost destroyed both of them. Now they exist in an armed-to-the-teeth neutrality that neither dare violate. The moment we set foot aboard the ship we are on Darkhan territory. There is no extradition agreement between the planets. Cassylia may want us – but not badly enough to start another war.'

That was all the explanation there was time for. Kerk swung the car out of the rush of traffic and on to a bridge marked *Official Cars Only*. Jason had a feeling of nakedness as they rolled under the harsh port lights towards the guarded gate ahead.

It was closed.

Another car approached the gate from the inside and Kerk slowed their car to a crawl. One of the guards talked to the driver of the car inside the port, then waved to the gate attendant. The barrier gate began to swing inward and Kerk jammed down on the accelerator.

Everything happened at once. The turbine howled, the spinning tyres screeched on the road and the car crashed open the gate. Jason had a vanishing glimpse of the open-mouthed guards, then they were skidding around the corner of a building. A few shots popped after them, but none came close.

Driving with one hand, Kerk reached under the dash and pulled out a gun that was the twin of the monster strapped to his arm. 'Use this instead of your own,' he said. 'Rocket-propelled explosive slugs. Make a great bang. Don't bother shooting at anyone – I'll take care of that. Just stir up a little action and make them keep their distance. Like this.'

He fired a single snapshot out the side-window and passed the gun to Jason almost before the slug hit. An empty truck blew up with a roar, raining pieces on the cars around and sending their drivers fleeing in panic.

After that it was a nightmare ride through a madhouse. Kerk drove with an apparent contempt for violent death. Other cars followed them and were lost in wheel-raising turns.

25

They careened almost the full length of the field, leaving a trail of smoking chaos.

Then the pursuit was all behind them and the only thing ahead was the slim spire of the *Pride of Darkhan.*

The *Pride* was surrounded by a strong wire fence as suited the begruding status of her planetary origin. The gate was closed and guarded by soldiers with levelled guns, waiting for a shot at the approaching car. Kerk made no attempt to come near them. Instead he fed the last reserves of power to the car and headed for the fence. 'Cover your face,' he shouted.

Jason put his arms in front of his head just as they hit.

Torn metal screamed, the fence buckled, wrapped itself around the car, but did not break. Jason flew off the seat and into the padded dash. By the time Kerk had the warped door open, he realized that the ride was over. Kerk must have seen the spin of his eyeballs because he didn't talk, just pulled Jason out and threw him on to the hood of the ruined car.

'Climb over the buckled wire and make a run for the ship,' he shouted.

If there was any doubt what he meant, he set Jason an example of fine roadwork. It was inconceivable that someone of his bulk could run so fast, yet he did. He moved more like a charging tank than a man. Jason shook the fog from his head and worked up some speed himself. Nevertheless, he was barely half-way to the ship when Kerk hit the gangway. It was already unhooked from the ship, but the shocked attendants stopped rolling it away as the big man bounded up the steps.

At the top he turned and fired at the soldiers who were charging in through the open gate. They dropped, crawled, and returned his fire. Very few shot at Jason's running form.

The scene in front of Jason cranked over in slow motion. Kerk standing at the top of the ramp, coolly returning the fire that splashed all about. He could have found safety in an instant through the open port behind him. The only reason he stayed there was to cover Jason.

'Thanks,' Jason managed to gasp as he made the last few steps up the gangway, jumped the gap and collapsed inside the ship.

'You're perfectly welcome,' Kerk said as he joined him, waving his gun to cool it off.

A grim-jawed ship's officer stood back out of range of fire from the ground and looked them both up and down. 'And just what the hell is going on here?' he growled.

Kerk tested the barrel with a wet thumb, then let the gun slide back into its holster. 'We are law-abiding citizens of a different system who have committed no criminal acts. The savages of Cassylia are too barbarous for civilized company. Therefore we are going to Darkhan – here are our tickets – in whose sovereign territory I believe we are at this moment.' This last was added for the benefit of the Cassylian officer who had just stumbled to the top of the gangway and was raising his gun.

The soldier couldn't be blamed. He saw these badly wanted criminals getting away. Aboard a Darkhan ship as well. Anger got the best of him and he brought his gun up.

'Come out of there, you scum! You're not escaping that easily. Come out slowly with your hands up or I'll blast you . . .'

It was a frozen moment of time that stretched and stretched without breaking. The pistol covered Kerk and Jason. Neither of them attempted to reach for their own guns.

The gun twitched a bit as the ship's officer moved, then steadied back on the two men. The Darkhan spaceman hadn't gone far, just a pace across the lock. This was enough to bring him next to a red box set flush with the wall. With a single, swift gesture, he flipped up the cover and poised his thumb over the button inside. When he smiled, his lips peeled back to show all his teeth. He had made up his mind, and it was the arrogance of the Cassylian officer that had been the deciding factor.

'Fire a single shot into Darkhan territory and I press this button,' he shouted. 'And you know what this button does – every one of your ships has them as well. Commit a hostile act against this ship and *someone* will press a button. Every control rod will be blown out of the ship's pile at that instant and half your filthy city will go up in the explosion.' His smile was chiselled on his face and there was no doubt he would do what he said. 'Go ahead, fire. I think I would enjoy pressing this.'

The take-off siren was hooting now, the *close lock* light blinking an angry message from the bridge. Like four actors in a grim drama, they faced each other an instant more.

Then the Cassylian officer, growling with unvoiceable, frustrated anger, turned and leaped back to the steps.

'All passengers board ship. Forty-five seconds to take-off. Clear the port.' The ship's officer slammed shut the cover of the box and locked it as he talked. There was barely time to make the acceleration couches before the *Pride of Darkhan* cleared ground.

CHAPTER FIVE

Once the ship was in orbit, the captain sent for Jason and Kerk. Kerk took the floor and was completely frank about the previous night's activities. The only fact of importance he left out was Jason's background as a professional gambler. He drew a beautiful picture of two lucky strangers whom the evil forces of Cassylia wanted to deprive of their gambling profits. All this fitted perfectly the captain's preconception of Cassylia. In the end, he congratulated his officer on the correctness of his actions and began the preparation of a long report to his government. He gave the two men his best wishes as well as the liberty of the ship.

It was a short trip. Jason barely had time to catch up on his sleep before they grounded on Darkhan. Being without luggage, they were the first ones through customs. They left the shed just in time to see another ship landing in a distant pit. Kerk stopped to watch it and Jason followed his gaze. It was a grey, scarred ship. With the stubby lines of a freighter – but sporting as many large guns as a cruiser.

'Yours, of course,' Jason said.

Kerk nodded and started towards the ship. One of the locks opened as they came up but no one appeared. Instead a remote-release folding ladder rattled down to the ground. Kerk swarmed up it and Jason followed glumly. Somehow, he felt, this was overdoing the no-frills-and-nonsense attitude.

Jason was catching on to Pyrran ways, though. The reception aboard ship for the ambassador was just what he expected. Nothing. Kerk closed the lock himself and they found couches as the take-off horn sounded. The main jets roared and acceleration smashed down on Jason.

It didn't stop. Instead it grew stronger, squeezing the air out of his lungs and the sight from his eyes. He screamed but couldn't hear his own voice through the roaring in his ears. Mercifully he blacked out.

When consciousness returned the ship was at zero-G. Jason kept his eyes closed and let the pain seep out of his body. Kerk spoke suddenly; he was standing next to the couch.

'My fault, Meta, I should have told you we had a one-G passenger aboard. You might have eased up a bit on your usual bone-breaking take-off.'

'It doesn't seem to have harmed him much – but what's he doing here?'

Jason felt mild surprise that the second voice was a girl's. But he wasn't interested enough to go to the trouble of opening his sore eyes.

'Going to Pyrrus. I tried to talk him out of it, of course, but I couldn't change his mind. It's a shame, too, I would like to have done more for him. He's the one who got the money for us.'

'Oh, that's awful,' the girl said. Jason wondered why it was *awful*. It didn't make sense to his groggy mind. 'It would have been much better if he had stayed on Darkhan,' the girl continued. 'He's very nice-looking. I think it's a shame he has to die.'

That was too much for Jason. He pried one eye open, then the other. The voice belonged to a girl of about twenty-one who was standing next to the bed, gazing down at Jason. She was beautiful.

Jason's eyes opened wider as he realized she was *very* beautiful – with the kind of beauty he had never found on the planets in the centre of the galaxy. The women he had known all ran to pale skin, hollow shoulders, grey faces covered with tints and dyes. They were the product of centuries of breeding weak-

29

nesses back into the race, as the advance of medicine kept alive more and more non-survival types.

This girl was the direct opposite in every way. She was the product of survival on Pyrrus. The heavy gravity that produced bulging muscles in man, brought out firm strength in strap-like female muscles. She had the taut figure of a goddess, tanned skin and perfectly formed face. Her hair, which was cut short, circled her head with a golden crown. The only unfeminine thing about her was the gun she wore in a bulky forearm holster. When she saw Jason's eyes open she smiled at him. Her teeth were as even and as white as he had expected.

'I'm Meta, pilot of this ship. And you must be –'

'Jason dinAlt. That was a lousy take-off, Meta.'

'I'm really very sorry,' she laughed. 'But being born on a two-G planet makes you a little immune to acceleration. I save fuel too, with the synergy curve –'

Kerk gave a noncommittal grunt. 'Come along, Meta, we'll take a look at the cargo. Some of the new stuff will plug the gaps in the perimeter.'

'Oh, yes,' she said, almost clapping her hands with happiness. 'I read the specs, they're simply wonderful.'

Like a schoolgirl with a new dress. Or a box of candy. That's a great attitude to have towards bombs and flame-throwers. Jason smiled wryly at the thought as he groaned off the couch. The two Pyrrans had gone and he pulled himself painfully through the door after them.

It took him a long time to find his way to the hold. The ship was big and apparently empty of crew. Jason finally found a man sleeping in one of the brightly lit cabins. He recognized him as the driver who had turned the car over to them on Cassylia. The man, who had been sleeping soundly a moment before, opened his eyes as soon as Jason drifted into the room. He was wide awake.

'How do I get to the cargo hold?' Jason asked.

The other told him, closed his eyes and went instantly back to sleep before Jason could even say thanks.

In the hold, Kerk and Meta had opened some of the crates and were chortling with joy over their lethal contents. Meta, a pressure cannister in her arms, turned to Jason as he came through the door.

'Just look at this,' she said. 'This powder in here – why, you can eat it like dirt, with less harm. Yet it is instantly deadly to all forms of vegetable life. . . .' She stopped suddenly as she realized Jason didn't share her extreme pleasure. 'I'm sorry. Only I forgot for a moment there that you weren't a Pyrran. So you don't really understand, do you?'

Before he could answer, the PA speaker called her name.

'Jump time,' she said. 'Come with me to the bridge while I do the equations. We can talk there. I know so little about any place except Pyrrus that I have a million questions to ask.'

Jason followed her to the bridge where she relieved the duty officer and began taking readings for the jump setting. She looked out of place among the machines, a sturdy but supple figure in a simple, one-piece shipsuit. Yet there was no denying the efficiency with which she went about her job.

'Meta, aren't you a little young to be the pilot of an inter-stellar ship?'

'Am I?' She thought for a second. 'I really don't know how old pilots are supposed to be. I have been piloting for about three years now and I'm almost twenty. Is that younger than usual?'

Jason opened his mouth – then laughed. 'I suppose that all depends on what planet you're from. Some places you would have trouble getting licensed. But I'll bet things are different on Pyrrus. By their standards you must rank as an old lady.'

'Now, you're making a joke,' Meta said serenely as she fed a figure into the calculator. 'I've seen old ladies on some planets. They are wrinkled and have grey hair. I don't know how old they are, I asked one but she wouldn't tell me her age. But I'm sure they must be older than anyone on Pyrrus, no one looks like that there.'

'I don't mean old that way,' Jason groped for the right word. 'Not old – but grown-up, mature. An adult.'

'Everyone is grown-up,' she answered. 'At least soon after they leave the wards. And they do that when they're six. My first child is grown-up, and the second one would be too, only he's dead. So I *surely* must be.'

31

That seemed to settle the question for her, though Jason's thoughts jumped with the alien concepts and background inherent behind her words.

Meta punched in the last setting, and the course tape began to chunk out of the case. She turned her attention back to Jason. 'I'm glad you're aboard this trip, though I am sorry you are going to Pyrrus. But we'll have lots of time to talk and there are so many things I want to find out. About other planets. And why people go around acting the way they do. Not at all like home where you *know* why people are doing things all the time.' She frowned over the tape for a moment, then turned her attention back to Jason. 'What is your home planet like?'

One after another the usual lies he told people came to his lips, and were pushed away. Why bother lying to a girl who really didn't care if you were serf or noble? To her there were only two kinds of people in the galaxy. Pyrrans, and the rest. For the first time since he had fled from Porgorstorsaand, he found himself telling someone the truth of his origin.

'My home planet? Just about the stuffiest, dullest, dead-end in the universe. You can't believe the destructive decay of a planet that is mainly agrarian, caste-conscious and completely satisfied with its own boring existence. Not only is there no change – but no one *wants* change. My father was a farmer, so I should have been a farmer too – if I had listened to the advice of my betters. It was unthinkable, as well as forbidden, for me to do anything else. And everything I wanted to do was against the law. I was fifteen before I learned to read – out of a book stolen from a noble school. After that there was no turning back. By the time I stowed away aboard an off-world freighter at nineteen I must have broken every law on the planet. Happily. Leaving home for me was just like getting out of prison.'

Meta shook her head at the thought. 'I just can't imagine a place like that. But I'm sure I wouldn't like it there.'

'I'm sure you wouldn't,' Jason smiled. 'So once I was in space, with no law-abiding talents or skills, I just wandered into one thing and another. In this age of technology, I was completely out of place. Oh, I suppose I could have done well in some army, but I'm not so good at taking orders. Whenever I gambled I did well, so little by little I just drifted into it. People are the same everywhere, so I manage to make out very well wherever I end up.'

'I know what you mean about people being alike, but they are so *different*,' she said. 'I'm not being clear at all, am I? What I mean is that at home I know what people will do and why they do it at the same time. People on all the other planets do act alike, as you said, yet I have very much trouble understanding why. For instance, I like to try the local food when we set down on a planet, and if there is time I always do. There are bars and restaurants near every spaceport so I go there. And I always have trouble with the men. They want to buy me drinks, hold my hand.'

'Well, a single girl in those port joints has to expect a certain amount of interest from the men.'

'Oh, I know that,' she said. 'What I don't understand is why they don't listen when I tell them I am not interested and to go away. They just laugh and pull up a chair, usually. But I have found that one thing works wherever I am. I tell them if they don't stop bothering me I'll break their arm.'

'Does that stop them?' Jason asked.

'No, of course not. But after I break their arm they go away. And the others don't bother me either. It's a lot of fuss to go through and the food is usually awful.'

Jason didn't laugh. Particularly when he realized that this girl *could* break the arm of any spaceport thug in the galaxy. She was a strange mixture of naïveté and strength, unlike anyone he had ever met before. Once again he realized that he *had* to visit the planet that produced people like her and Kerk.

'Tell me about Pyrrus,' he asked. 'Why is it that you and Kerk assume automatically that I will drop dead as soon as I land? What is the planet like?'

All the warmth was gone from her face now. 'I can't tell you. You will have to see for yourself. I know that much after visiting some of the other worlds. Pyrrus is like nothing you galaxy people have ever experienced. You won't really believe it until it is too late. Will you promise me something?'

'No,' he answered. 'At least not until after I hear what it is and decide.'

'Don't leave the ship when we land. You should be safe

enough aboard, and I'll be flying a cargo out within a few weeks.'

'I'll promise nothing of the sort. I'll leave when I want to leave.' Jason knew there was undoubtedly a reason for her words, but he resented her automatic superiority.

Meta finished the jump settings without another word. There was a tension in the room that prevented them both from talking.

It was the next shipday before he saw her again, and then it was completely by accident. She was in the astrogation dome when he entered, looking up at the spark-filled blackness of the jump sky. For the first time he saw her off duty, wearing something other than a shipsuit. This was a thin and softly shining robe that clung to her body.

She smiled at him. 'The stars are so wonderful. Come see.' Jason stood close to her, looking up. The oddly geometric patterns of the jump sky were familiar to him, yet they still had the power to draw him forward. Even more so now. Meta's presence made a disturbing difference in the dark silence of the dome. Her tilted head almost rested on his shoulder, the crown of her hair eclipsing part of the sky, the smell of it soft in his nostrils.

Almost without thought his arms went around her, aware of the warm firmness of her flesh beneath the thin robe. She did not resent it, for she covered his hands with hers.

'You're smiling,' she said. 'You like the stars too.'

'Very much,' he answered. 'But more than that. I remembered the story you told me. Do you want to break my arm, Meta?'

'Of course not,' she said very seriously, then smiled back. 'I like you, Jason. Even though you're not a Pyrran, I like you very much. And I've been so lonely.'

When she looked up at him, he kissed her. She returned the kiss with a passion that had no shame or false modesty.

'My cabin is just down this corridor,' she said.

34

CHAPTER SIX

After that they were together constantly. When Meta was on duty he brought her meals to the bridge and they talked. Jason learned little more about her world since, by unspoken agreement, they didn't discuss it. He talked of the many planets he had visited and the people he had known. She was an appreciative listener and the time went quickly by. They enjoyed each other's company and it was a wonderful trip.

Then it ended.

There were fourteen people aboard the ship, yet Jason had never seen more than two or three at a time. There was a fixed rotation of duties that they followed in the ship's operation. When not on duty, the Pyrrans minded their own business in an intense and self-sufficient manner. Only when the ship came out of jump and the PA barked *assembly* did they all get together.

Kerk was giving orders for the landing and questions were snapped back and forth. It was all technical and Jason didn't bother following it. It was the attitude of the Pyrrans that drew his attention. Their talk tended to be faster now as were their motions. They were like soldiers preparing for battle.

Their sameness struck Jason for the first time. Not that they looked alike or did the same things. It was the *way* they moved and reacted that caused the striking similarity. They were like great, stalking cats. Walking fast, tense and ready to spring at all times, their eyes never still for an instant.

Jason tried to talk to Meta after the meeting, but she was almost a stranger. She answered in monosyllables and her eyes never met his, just brushed over them and went on. There was nothing he could really say, so she moved to leave. He started to put his hand out to stop her – then thought better of it. There would be other times to talk.

Kerk was the only one who took any notice of him – and then only to order him to an acceleration couch.

Meta's landings were infinitely worse than her take-offs. At least when she landed on Pyrrus. There were sudden acceleration surges in every direction. At one point there was a free fall that seemed endless. There were loud thuds against the hull that shook the framework of the ship. It was more like a battle than a landing and Jason wondered how much truth there was in that.

When the ship finally landed, Jason didn't even know it. The constant two-G's felt like deceleration. Only the descending moan of the ship's engines convinced him they were down. Unbuckling the straps and sitting up was an effort.

Two-G's didn't seem that bad. At first. Walking required the same exertion as would carrying a man of his own weight on his shoulders. When Jason lifted his arm to unlatch the door it was as heavy as two arms. He shuffled slowly towards the main lock.

They were all there ahead of him, two of the men rolling transparent cylinders from a near-by room. From their obvious weight and the way they clanged when they bumped, Jason knew they were made of transparent metal. He couldn't conceive any possible use for them. Empty cylinders a metre in diameter, longer than a man. One end solid, the other hinged and sealed. It wasn't until Kerk spun the sealing wheel and opened one of them that their use became apparent.

'Get in,' Kerk said. 'When you're locked inside, you'll be carried out of the ship.'

'Thank you, no,' Jason told him. 'I have no particular desire to make a spectacular landing on your planet sealed up like a packaged sausage.'

'Don't be a fool,' was Kerk's snapped answer. 'We're *all* going out in these tubes. We've been away too long to risk the surface without reorientation.'

Jason did feel a little foolish as he saw the others getting into tubes. He picked the nearest one, slid into it feet first, and pulled the lid closed. When he tightened the wheel in the centre, it squeezed down against a flexible seal. Within a minute the CO_2 content in the closed cylinder went up and an air regenerator at the bottom hummed into life.

Kerk was the last one in. He checked the seals on all the other tubes first, then jabbed the airlock override release. As it started cycling, he quickly sealed himself in the remaining cylinder. Both inner and outer locks ground slowly open and dim light filtered in through sheets of falling rain.

For Jason, the whole thing seemed an anticlimax. All this preparation for absolutely nothing. Long, impatient minutes passed before a lift truck appeared driven by a Pyrran. He loaded the cylinders on to his truck like so much dead cargo. Jason had the misfortune to be buried at the bottom of the pile so could see absolutely nothing when they drove outside.

It wasn't until the man-carrying cylinders had been dumped in a metal-walled room, that Jason saw his first native Pyrran life.

The lift-truck driver was swinging a thick outer door shut when something flew in through the entrance and struck against the far wall. Jason's eye was caught by the motion; he looked to see what it was when it dropped straight down towards his face.

Forgetful of the metal cylinder wall, he flinched away. The creature struck the transparent metal and clung to it. Jason had the perfect opportunity to examine it in every detail.

It was almost too horrible to be believable. As though it were a bearer of death stripped to the very essentials. A mouth that split the head in two, rows of teeth, serrated and pointed. Leathery, claw-tipped wings, longer claws on the limbs that tore at the metal wall.

Terror rose up in Jason, as he saw that the claws were tearing gouges in the transparent metal. Wherever the creature's saliva touched, the metal clouded and chipped under the assault of the teeth.

Logic said these were just scratches on the thick tube. They couldn't matter. But blind, unreasoning fear sent Jason curling away as far as he could. Shrinking inside himself, seeking escape.

Only when the flying creature began dissolving did he realize the nature of the room outside. Sprays of steaming liquid came from all sides, raining down until the cylinders were covered. After one last clash of its jaws, the Pyrran animal was washed off and carried away. The liquid drained away through the floor and a second and third shower followed.

While the solutions were being pumped away, Jason fought

37

to bring his emotions into line. He was surprised at himself. No matter how frightful the creature had been, he couldn't understand the fear it could generate through the wall of the sealed tube. His reaction was all out of proportion to the cause. Even with the creature destroyed and washed out of sight, it took all of his will power to steady his nerves and bring his breathing back to normal.

Meta walked by outside and he realized the sterilization process was finished. He opened his own tube and climbed wearily out. Meta and the others had gone by this time and only a hawk-faced stranger remained, waiting for him.

'I'm Brucco, in charge of the adaptation clinic. Kerk told me who you were, I'm sorry you're here. Now come along, I want some blood samples.'

'Now I feel right at home,' Jason said. 'The old Pyrran hospitality.' Brucco only grunted and stamped out. Jason followed him down a bare corridor into a sterile lab.

The double gravity was tiring, a constant drag on sore muscles. While Brucco ran tests on the blood sample, Jason rested. He had almost dozed off into a painful sleep when Brucco returned with a tray of bottles and hypodermic needles.

'Amazing,' he announced. 'Not an antibody in your serum that would be of any use on this planet. I have a batch of antigens here that will make you sick as a beast for at least a day. Take off your shirt.'

'Have you done this often?' Jason asked. 'I mean juice up an outlander so he can enjoy the pleasures of your world?'

Brucco jabbed in a needle that felt like it grated on the bone. 'Not often at all. Last time was years ago. A half-dozen researchers from some institute, willing to pay well for the chance to study the local life forms. We didn't say no. Always need more galaxy currency.'

Jason was already beginning to feel lightheaded from the shots. 'How many of them lived?' he mumbled vaguely.

'One. We got him off in time. Made them pay in advance, of course.'

At first Jason thought the Pyrran was joking. Then he remembered they had very little interest in humour of any kind. If one half of what Meta and Kerk had told him was true, six-to-one odds weren't bad at all.

There was a bed in the next room and Brucco helped him to it. Jason felt drugged and probably was. He fell into a deep sleep and into the dream.

Fear and hatred. Mixed in equal parts and washed over him red hot. If this was a dream, he never wanted to sleep again. If it wasn't a dream, he wanted to die. He tried to fight up against it, but only sank in more deeply. There was no beginning and no end to the fear and no way to escape.

When consciousness returned, Jason could remember no detail of the nightmare. Just the fear remained. He was soaked with sweat and ached in every muscle. It must have been the massive dose of shots, he finally decided, that and the brutal gravity. That didn't take the taste of fear out of his mouth, though.

Brucco stuck his head in the door then and looked Jason up and down. 'Thought you were dead,' he said. 'Slept the clock around. Don't move, I'll get something to pick you up.'

The pickup was in the form of another needle and a glassful of evil-looking fluid. It settled his thirst, but made him painfully aware of a gnawing hunger.

'Want to eat?' Brucco asked. 'I'll bet you do. I've speeded up your metabolism so you'll build muscle faster. Only way you'll ever beat the gravity. Give you quite an appetite for a while though.'

Brucco ate at the same time and Jason had a chance to ask some questions. 'When do I get a chance to look around your fascinating planet? So far this trip has been about as interesting as a jail term.'

'Relax and enjoy your food. Probably be months before you're able to go outside. If at all.'

Jason felt his jaw hanging and closed it with a snap. 'Could you possibly tell me why?'

'Of course. You will have to go through the same training course that our children take. It takes them six years. Of course, it's their first six years of life. So you might think that you, as an adult, could learn faster. Then again, they have the advantage of heredity. All I can say is you'll go outside these sealed buildings when you're ready.'

Brucco had finished eating while he talked, and sat staring

at Jason's bare arms with growing disgust. 'The first thing we want to get you is a gun,' he said. 'It gives me a sick feeling to see someone without one.'

Of course Brucco wore his own gun continually, even within the sealed buildings.

'Every gun is fitted to its owner and would be useless on anyone else,' Brucco said. 'I'll show you why.' He led Jason to an armoury jammed with deadly weapons. 'Put your arm in this while I make the adjustments.'

It was a box-like machine with a pistol grip on the side. Jason clutched the grip and rested his elbow on a metal loop. Brucco fixed pointers that touched his arm, then copied the results from the meters. Reading the figures from his list, he selected various components from bins and quickly assembled a power holster and gun. With the holster strapped to his forearm and the gun in his hand, Jason noticed for the first time they were connected by a flexible cable. The gun fitted his hand perfectly.

'This is the secret of the power holster,' Brucco said, tapping the flexible cable. 'It is perfectly loose while you are using the weapon. But when you want it returned to the holster –' Brucco made an adjustment and the cable became a stiff rod that whipped the gun from Jason's hand and suspended it in mid air.

'Then the return.' The rod cable whirred and snapped the gun back into the holster. 'The drawing action is the opposite of this, of course.'

'A great gadget,' Jason said. 'But how *do* I draw? Do I whistle or something for the gun to pop out?'

'No, it is not sonic control,' Brucco answered with a sober face. 'It is much more precise than that. Here, take your left hand and grasp an imaginary gun butt. Tense your trigger finger. Do you notice the pattern of the tendons in the wrist? Sensitive actuators touch the tendons in your right wrist. They ignore all patterns except the one that says *hand ready to receive gun.* After a time the mechanism becomes completely automatic. When you want the gun, it is in your hand. When you don't, it is in the holster.'

Jason made grasping motions with his right hand, crooked his index finger. There was a sudden, smashing pain against his

40

hand and a loud roar. The gun was in his hand – half the fingers were numb – and smoke curled up from the barrel.

'Of course, there are only blank charges in the gun until you learn control. Guns are *always* loaded. There is no safety. Notice the lack of a trigger guard. That enables you to bend your trigger finger a slight bit more when drawing so the gun will fire the instant it touches your hand.'

It was without doubt the most murderous weapon Jason had ever handled, as well as being the hardest to manage. Working against the muscle-burning ache of high gravity, he fought to control the devilish device. It had an infuriating way of vanishing into the holster just as he was about to pull the trigger. Even worse was the tendency to leap out before he was quite ready. The gun went to the position where his hand should be. If the fingers weren't correctly placed, they were crashed aside. Jason only stopped the practice when his entire hand was one livid bruise.

Complete mastery would come with time, but he could already understand why the Pyrrans never removed their guns. It would be like removing a part of your own body. The movement of gun from holster to hand was too fast for him to detect. It was certainly faster than the neural current that shaped the hand into the gun-holding position. For all apparent purposes it was like having a lightning bolt in your fingertip. Point the finger and blamm, there's the explosion.

Brucco had left Jason to practise alone. When his aching hand could take no more, he stopped and headed back towards his own quarters. Turning a corner, he had a quick glimpse of a familiar figure going away from him.

'Meta! Wait for a second! I want to talk to you.'

She turned impatiently as he shuffled up, going as fast as he could in the doubled gravity. Everything about her seemed different from the girl he had known on the ship. Heavy boots came as high as her knees, her figure was lost in bulky coveralls of some metallic fabric. The trim waist was bulged out by a belt of canisters. Her very expression was coldly distant.

'I've missed you,' he said. 'I hadn't realized you were in this building.' He reached for her hand but she moved it out of his reach.

'What is it you want?' she asked.

'What is it I want!' he echoed with barely concealed anger. 'This is Jason, remember me? We're friends. It *is* allowed for friends to talk without "wanting" anything.'

'What happened on the ship has nothing to do with what happens on Pyrrus.' She started forward impatiently as she talked. 'I have finished my reconditioning and must return to work. You'll be staying here in the sealed buildings so I won't be seeing you.'

'Why don't you stay with the rest of the children – that's what your tone implies. And don't try walking out, there are some things we have to settle first –'

Jason made the mistake of putting out his hand to stop her. He didn't really know what happened next. One instant he was standing – the next he sprawled suddenly on the floor. His shoulder was badly bruised, and Meta had vanished down the corridor.

Limping back to his own room, he muttered curses under his breath. Dropping on to his rock-hard bed, he tried to remember the reasons that had brought him here in the first place. And weighed them against the perpetual torture of the gravity, the fear-filled dreams it inspired, the automatic contempt of these people for any outsider. He quickly checked the growing tendency to feel sorry for himself. By Pyrran standards, he *was* soft and helpless. If he wanted them to think any better of him, he would have to change a good deal.

He sank into a fatigue-drugged sleep then, that was broken only by the screaming fear of his dreams.

CHAPTER SEVEN

In the morning, Jason awoke with a bad headache and the feeling he had never been to sleep. As he took some of the carefully portioned stimulants that Brucco had given him, he wondered again about the combination of factors that filled his sleep with such horror.

'Eat quickly,' Brucco told him when they met in the dining-room. 'I can no longer spare you time for individual instruction.

You will join the regular classes and take the prescribed courses. Only come to me if there is some special problem that the instructors or trainers can't handle.'

The classes, as Jason should have expected, were composed of stern-faced little children. With their compact bodies and no-nonsense mannerisms, they were recognizably Pyrran. But they were still children enough to consider it very funny to have an adult in their classes. Jammed behind one of the tiny desks, the red-faced Jason did not think it was much of a joke.

All resemblance to a normal school ended with the physical form of the classroom. For one thing, every child – no matter how small – packed a gun. And the courses were all involved with survival. The only possible grade in a curriculum like this was hundred per cent and students stayed with a lesson until they had mastered it perfectly. No courses were offered in the normal scholastic subjects. Presumably these were studied after the child graduated survival school and could face the world alone. Which was a logical and cold-blooded way of looking at things. In fact, logical and cold-blooded could describe any Pyrran activity.

Most of the morning was spent on the operation of one of the medikits that strapped around the waist. This was an infection and poison analyser that was pressed over a puncture wound. If any toxins were present, the antidote was automatically injected on the site. Simple in operation but incredibly complex in construction. Since all Pyrrans serviced their own equipment – you could then only blame yourself if it failed – they had to learn the construction and repair of all the devices. Jason did much better than the child students, though the effort exhausted him.

In the afternoon, he had his first experience with a training machine. His instructor was a twelve-year-old boy, whose cold voice didn't conceal his contempt for the soft off-worlder.

'All the training machines are physical duplicates of the real surface of the planet, corrected constantly as the life forms change. The only difference between them is the varying degree of deadliness. This first machine you will use is of course the one infants are put into –'

'You're too kind,' Jason murmured. 'Your flattery over-

43

whelms me.' The instructor continued, taking no notice of the interruptions.

'– infants are put into it as soon as they can crawl. It is real in substance, though completely de-activated.'

Training machine was the wrong word, Jason realized as they entered through the thick door. This was a chunk of the outside world duplicated in an immense chamber. It took very little suspension of reality for him to forget the painted ceiling and artificial sun high above and imagine himself outdoors at last. The scene *seemed* peaceful enough. Though clouds banking on the horizon threatened a violent Pyrran storm.

'You must wander around and examine things,' the instructor told Jason. 'Whenever you touch something with your hand, you will be told about it. Like this . . .'

The boy bent over and pushed his finger against a blade of the soft grass that covered the ground. Immediately a voice barked from hidden speakers.

'Poison grass. Boots to be worn at all times.'

Jason kneeled and examined the grass. The blade was tipped with a hard, shiny hook. He realized with a start that every single blade of grass was the same. The soft green lawn was a carpet of death. As he straightened up, he glimpsed something under a broad-leaved plant. A crouching, scale-covered animal, whose tapered head terminated in a long spike.

'What's *that* in the bottom of my garden?' he asked. 'You certainly give the babies pleasant playmates,' Jason turned and realized he was talking to the air; the instructor was gone. He shrugged and petted the scaly monstrosity.

'Horndevil,' the impersonal voice said from mid-air. 'Clothing and shoes no protection. Kill it.'

A sharp *crack* shattered the silence as Jason's gun went off. The horndevil fell over on its side, keyed to react to the blank charge.

'Well – I *am* learning,' Jason said, and the thought pleased him. The words *kill it* had been used by Brucco while teaching him to use the gun. Their stimulus had reached an unconscious level. He was aware of wanting to shoot only after he had heard the shot. His respect for Pyrran training techniques went up.

Jason spent a thoroughly unpleasant afternoon wandering in

the child's garden of horror. Death was everywhere. While all the time the disembodied voice gave him stern advice in simple language. So he could do unto, rather than being done in. He had never realized that violent death could come in so many repulsive forms. *Everything* here was deadly to man – from the smallest insect to the largest plant.

Such singleness of purpose seemed completely unnatural. Why was this planet so alien to human life? He made a mental note to ask Brucco. Meanwhile he tried to find one life form that wasn't out for his blood. He didn't succeed. After a long search, he found the only thing that when touched didn't elicit deadly advice. This was a chunk of rock that projected from a meadow of poison grass. Jason sat on it with a friendly feeling and pulled his feet up. An oasis of peace. Some minutes passed while he rested his gravity-weary body.

'ROTFUNGUS! DO NOT TOUCH!'

The voice blasted at twice its normal volume and Jason leaped as if he had been shot. The gun was in his hand, nosing about for a target. Only when he bent over and looked closely at the rock where he had been sitting, did he understand. There were flaky grey patches that hadn't been there when he sat down.

'Oh, you tricky devils!' he shouted at the machine. 'How many kids have you frightened off that rock after they thought they had found a little peace!' He resented the snide bit of conditioning, but respected it at the same time. Pyrrans learned very early in life that there was no safety on this planet – except that which they provided for themselves.

While he was learning about Pyrrus, he was gaining new insight into the Pyrrans as well.

CHAPTER EIGHT

Days turned into weeks in the school, cut off from the world outside. Jason almost became proud of his ability to deal with death. He recognized all the animals and plants in the nursery room and had been promoted to a trainer where the beasts made sluggish charges at him. His gun picked off the attackers with dull regularity. The constant, daily classes were beginning to bore him as well.

Though the gravity still dragged at him, his muscles were making great efforts to adjust. After the daily classes, he no longer collapsed immediately into bed. Only the nightmares became worse. He had finally mentioned them to Brucco, who mixed up a sleeping potion that took away most of their effect. The dreams were still there, but Jason was only vaguely aware of them upon awakening.

By the time Jason had mastered all the gadgetry that kept the Pyrrans alive, he had graduated to a most realistic trainer that was only a hairsbreadth away from the real thing. The difference was just in quality. The insect poisons caused swelling and pain instead of instant death. Animals could cause bruises and tear flesh, but stopped short of ripping off limbs. You couldn't get killed in this trainer, but could certainly come very close to it.

Jason wandered through this large and rambling jungle with the rest of the five-year-olds. There was something a bit humorous, yet sad, about their unchildlike grimness. Though they still might laugh in their quarters, they realized there was no laughing outside. To them survival was linked up with social acceptance and desirability. In this way Pyrrus was a simple black-and-white society. To prove your value to yourself and your world, you only had to stay alive. This had great importance in racial survival, but had very stultifying effects on individual personality. Children were turned into like-faced killers always on the alert to deal out death.

Some of the children graduated into the outside world and others took their places. Jason watched this process for a while before he realized that all of those from the original group he had entered with were gone. That same day he looked up the chief of the adaptation centre.

'Brucco,' Jason asked, 'how long do you plan to keep me in this kindergarten shooting gallery?'

'You're not being "kept" here,' Brucco told him in his usual irritated tone. 'You will be here until you qualify for the outside.'

'Which I have a funny feeling will be never. I can now field-strip and reassemble every one of your blasted gadgets in the dark. I am a dead shot with this cannon. At this present moment, if I had to, I could write a book on the Complete Flora and Fauna of Pyrrus, and How to Kill It. Perhaps I don't do as well as my six-year-old companions. But I have a hunch I do about as good a job now as I ever will. Is that true?'

Brucco squirmed with the effort to be evasive, yet didn't succeed. 'I think, that is, you know you weren't born here, and . . .'

'Come, come,' Jason said with glee. 'A straight-faced old Pyrran like you shouldn't try to lie to one of the weaker races that specialize in that sort of thing. It goes without saying that I'll always be sluggish with this gravity, as well as having other inborn handicaps. I admit that. We're not talking about that now. The question is, Will I improve with more training, or have I reached a peak of my own *development* now?'

Brucco sweated. 'With the passage of time there will be improvement, of course. . . .'

'Sly devil!' Jason waggled a finger at him. 'Yes or no, now. Will I improve *now* by more training *now*?'

'No,' Brucco said and still looked troubled. Jason sized him up like a poker hand.

'Now let's think about that. I won't improve, yet I'm still stuck here. That's no accident. So you must have been ordered to keep me here. And from what I have seen of this planet, admittedly very little, I would say that Kerk ordered you to keep me here. Is that right?'

'He was only doing it for your own sake,' Brucco explained. 'Trying to keep you alive.'

'The truth is out,' Jason said. 'So let us now forget about it. I didn't come here to shoot robots with your offspring. So please show me the street door. Or is there a graduating ceremony first? Speeches, handing out school pins, sabres overhead. . . .'

'Nothing like that,' Brucco snapped. 'I don't see how a grown man like you can talk such nonsense all the time. There is none of that, of course. Only some final work in the partial survival chamber. That is a compound that connects with the

47

outside – really is a part of the outside – except the most violent life forms are excluded. And even some of those manage to find their way in once in a while.'

'When do I go?' Jason shot the question.

'Tomorrow morning. Get a good night's sleep first. You'll need it.'

There was one bit of ceremony attendant with the graduation. When Jason came into his office in the morning, Brucco slid a heavy gunclip across the table.

'These are live bullets,' he said. 'I'm sure you'll be needing them. After this your gun will always be loaded.'

They came up to a heavy airlock, the only locked door Jason had seen in the centre. While Brucco unlocked it and threw the bolts, a sober-faced eight-year-old with a bandaged leg limped up.

'This is Grif,' Brucco said. 'He will stay with you, wherever you go, from now on.'

'My personal bodyguard?' Jason asked, looking down at the stocky child who barely reached his waist.

'You might call him that.' Brucco swung the door open. 'Grif tangled with a sawbird, so he won't be able to do any real work for a while. You yourself admitted that you will never be able to equal a Pyrran, so you should be glad of a little protection.'

'Always a kind word, that's you, Brucco,' Jason said. He bent over and shook hands with the boy. Even the eight-year-old had a bone-crushing grip.

The two of them entered the lock and Brucco swung the inner door shut behind them. As soon as it was sealed, the outer door opened automatically. It was only partly open when Grif's gun blasted twice. Then they stepped out on to the surface of Pyrrus, over the smoking body of one of its animals. Very symbolic, Jason thought. He was also bothered by the realization that not only hadn't he thought to look for something coming in, but he couldn't even identify the beast from its charred remains. He glanced around carefully, hoping he would be able to fire first next time.

This was an unfulfilled hope. The few beasts that came their way were always seen first by the boy. After an hour of this,

Jason was so irritated that he blasted an evil-looking thorn plant out of existence. He hoped that Grif wouldn't look too closely at it. Of course the boy did.

'That plant wasn't close. It is stupid to waste good ammunition on a plant,' Grif said.

There was no real trouble during the day. Jason ended by being bored, though soaked by the frequent rainstorms. If Grif was capable of carrying on a conversation, he didn't show it. All Jason's gambits failed. The following day went the same way. On the third day, Brucco appeared and looked Jason carefully up and down.

'I don't like to say it, but I suppose you are as ready to leave now as you ever will be. Change the virus-filter nose-plugs every day. Always check boots for tears and metal-cloth suiting for rips. Medikit supplies renewed once a week.'

'And wipe my nose and wear my galoshes. Anything else?' Jason asked.

Brucco started to say something, then changed his mind. 'Nothing that you shouldn't know well by now. Keep alert. And . . . good luck.' He followed up the words with a crushing handshake that was totally unexpected. As soon as the numbness left Jason's hand, he and Grif went out through the large entrance lock.

CHAPTER NINE

Real as they had been, the training chambers had not prepared him for the surface of Pyrrus. There was the basic similarity, of course. The feel of the poison grass underfoot and the erratic flight of a stingwing in the last instant before Grif blasted it. But these were scarcely noticeable in the crash of the elements around him.

A heavy rain was falling, more like a sheet of water than individual drops. Gusts of wind tore at it, hurling the deluge into his face. He wiped his eyes clear and could barely make out the conical forms of two volcanoes on the horizon, vomiting out clouds of smoke and flame. The reflection of this inferno was a sullen redness on the clouds that raced by in banks above them.

There was a rattle on his hard hat and something bounced off to splash to the ground. He bent over and picked up a hailstone as thick as his thumb. A sudden flurry of hail hammered painfully at his back and neck; he straightened hurriedly.

As quickly as it started, the storm was over. The sun burned down, melting the hailstones and sending curls of steam up from the wet street. Jason sweated inside his armoured clothing. Yet before he had gone a block, it was raining again and he shook with chill.

Grif trudged steadily along, indifferent either to the weather or the volcanoes that rumbled on the horizon and shook the ground beneath their feet. Jason tried to ignore his discomfort and match the boy's pace.

The walk was a depressing one. The heavy, squat buildings loomed greyly through the rain, more than half of them in ruins. They walked on a pedestrian way in the middle of the street. The occasional armoured trucks went by on both sides of them. The mid-street sidewalk puzzled Jason until Grif blasted something that hurtled out of a ruined building towards them. The central location gave them some chance to see what was coming. Suddenly Jason was very tired.

'I suppose there wouldn't be anything like a taxi on this planet,' he asked.

Grif just stared and frowned. It was obvious he had never even heard the word before. So they just trudged on, the boy holding himself back to Jason's slogging pace. Within half an hour, they had seen all he wanted to see.

'Grif, this city of yours is sure down at the heels. I hope the other ones are in better shape.'

'I don't know what you mean talking about heels. But there are no other cities. Some mining camps that can't be located inside the perimeter. But no other cities.'

This surprised Jason. He had always visualized the planet with more than one city. There were a *lot* of things he didn't know about Pyrrus, he realized suddenly. All of his efforts since landing had been taken up with the survival studies. There were a number of questions he wanted to ask – but of somebody other than his grouchy eight-year-old bodyguard. There was one person who would be best equipped to tell him what he wanted to know.

'Do you know Kerk?' he asked the boy. 'Apparently he's your ambassador to a lot of places but his last name —'

'Sure, everybody knows Kerk. But he's busy, you shouldn't see him.'

Jason shook a finger at him. 'Minder of my body you may be. But minder of my soul you are not. What do you say I call the shots and you go along to shoot the monsters. Okay?'

They took shelter from a sudden storm of fist-sized hailstones. Then, with ill grace, Grif led the way to one of the larger, central buildings. There were more people here and some of them even glanced at Jason for a minute, before turning back to their business. Jason dragged himself up two flights of stairs before they reached a door marked CO-ORDINATION AND SUPPLY.

'Kerk in here?' Jason asked.

'Sure,' the boy told him. 'He's in charge.'

'Fine. Now you get a nice cold drink or your lunch or something, and meet me back here in a couple of hours. I imagine Kerk can do as good a job of looking after me as you can.'

The boy stood doubtfully for a few seconds, then turned away. Jason wiped off some more sweat and pushed through the door.

There were a handful of people in the office beyond. None of them looked up at Jason or asked his business. Everything has a purpose on Pyrrus. If he came there, he must have had a good reason. No one would ever think to ask him what he wanted. Jason, used to the petty officialdom of a thousand worlds, waited for a few moments, before he understood. There was only one other door to the room, in the far wall. He shuffled over and opened it.

Kerk looked up from a desk strewn with papers and ledgers. 'I was wondering when you would show up,' he said.

'A lot sooner if you hadn't prevented it,' Jason told him as he dropped wearily into a chair. 'It finally dawned on me that I could spend the rest of my life in your bloodthirsty nursery school if I didn't do something about it. So here I am.'

'Ready to return to the "civilized" worlds, now that you've seen enough of Pyrrus?'

'I am not,' Jason said. 'And I'm getting very tired of everyone telling me to leave. I'm beginning to think that you and the rest of the Pyrrans are trying to hide something.'

Kerk smiled at the thought. 'What could we have to hide? I doubt if any planet has as simple and one-directional an existence as ours.'

'If that's true, then you certainly wouldn't mind answering a few direct questions about Pyrrus, would you?'

Kerk started to protest, then laughed. 'Well done. I should know better by now than to argue with you. What do you want to know?'

Jason tried to find a comfortable position on the hard chair, then gave up. 'What's the population of your planet?' he asked.

For a second Kerk hesitated, then said, 'Roughly thirty thousand. That's not very much for a planet that has been settled this long, but the reason for that is obvious.'

'All right, population thirty thousand,' Jason said. 'Now how about surface control of your planet? I was surprised to find out that this city within its protective wall – the perimeter – is the only one on the planet. Let's not consider the mining camps, since they are obviously just extensions of the city. Would you say then that you people control more or less of the planet's surface than you did in the past?'

Kerk picked up a length of steel pipe from the desk that he used as a paperweight and toyed with it as he thought. The thick steel bent like rubber at his touch as he concentrated on his answer.

'That's hard to say off-hand. There must be records of that sort of thing, though I wouldn't know where to find them. It depends on so many factors. . . .'

'Let's forget that for now then,' Jason said. 'I have another question that's really more relevant. Wouldn't you say that the population of Pyrrus is declining steadily, year after year?'

There was a sharp clang as the pipe struck the wall. Then Kerk was standing over Jason, his hands extended towards the smaller man, his face flushed and angry.

'Don't ever say that!' he roared. 'Don't let me ever hear you say that again!'

Jason sat as quietly as he could, talking slowly and picking out each word with care. His life hung in the balance.

'Don't get angry, Kerk. I meant no harm. I'm on your side, remember? I can talk to you because you've seen much more of the universe than the Pyrrans who have never left the planet. You are used to discussing things. You know that words are just symbols. We can talk and know you don't have to lose your temper over mere words. . . .'

Kerk slowly lowered his arms and stepped away. Then he turned and poured himself a glass of water from a bottle on the desk. He kept his back turned to Jason while he drank.

Very little of the sweat that Jason wiped from his sopping face was caused by the heat in the room.

'I'm – sorry I lost my temper,' Kerk said, dropping heavily into his chair. Doesn't usually happen. Been working hard lately, must have got my temper on edge.' He made no mention of what Jason had said.

'Happens to all of us,' Jason told him. 'I won't begin to describe the condition my nerves were in when I hit this planet. I'm finally forced to admit that everything you said about Pyrrus is true. It is the most deadly spot in the system. And only native-born Pyrrans could possibly survive here. I can manage to fumble along a bit after my training, but I know I would never stand a chance on my own. You probably know I have an eight-year-old as a bodyguard. Gives a good idea of my real status here.'

Anger suppressed, Kerk was back in control of himself now. His eyes narrowed in thought. 'Surprises me to hear you say that. Never thought I would hear you admit that anyone could be better than you at anything. Isn't that why you came here? To prove that you were as good as any native-born Pyrran?'

'Score one for your side,' Jason admitted. 'I didn't think it showed that much. And I'm glad to see your mind isn't as muscle-bound as your body. Yes, I'll admit that was probably my main reason for coming, that and curiosity.'

Kerk was following his own train of thought and puzzled where it was leading him. 'You came here to prove that you were as good as any native-born Pyrran. Yet now you admit that any eight-year-old can outdraw you. That just doesn't stack up with what I know about you. If you give with one hand, you must be taking back with the other. In what way do you still feel your natural superiority?' He asked it lightly, yet there was weight of tension behind his words.

Jason thought a long time before answering.

'I'll tell you,' he finally said. 'But don't snap my neck for it. I'm gambling that your civilized mind can control your reflexes. Because I have to talk about things that are strictly taboo on Pyrrus.

'In your people's eyes I'm a weakling because I come from off-world. Realize, though, that this is also my strength. I can see things that are hidden from you by long association. You know, the old business of not being able to see the forest for the trees in the way.'

Kerk nodded agreement and Jason went on. 'To continue the analogy further, I landed from an airship, and at first all I *could* see was the forest. To me certain facts are obvious. I think that you people know them too, only you keep your thoughts carefully repressed. They are hidden thoughts that are completely taboo. I'm going to tell you the biggest one of these secret thoughts and hope you can control yourself well enough not to kill me.'

Kerk's great hands tightened on the arms of the chair, the only sign he had heard. Jason spoke quietly, but his words penetrated as smoothly and easily as a lancet probing into a brain.

'I think human beings are losing the war on Pyrrus. After hundreds of years of occupation this is the only city on the planet – and it is half in ruins. As if it once had a larger population. That stunt we pulled off to get the shipload of war materials *was* a stunt. It might not have worked. And if it hadn't what would have happened to the city? You people are walking on the crumbling rim of a volcano and you won't admit it.'

Every muscle in Kerk's body was rigid as he sat stiffly in the chair, his face dotted with tiny beads of sweat. The slightest push too far and he would explode. Jason searched for a way to lessen some of the tension.

'I don't enjoy telling you these things. I'm doing it because I'm sure you know them already. You can't face these facts because you would then have to admit that all this fighting and killing is for absolutely no purpose. If your population is dropping steadily, then your fight is nothing but a particularly bloody form of racial suicide. You could leave this planet, but that would be admitting defeat. And I'm sure Pyrrans prefer death to defeat.'

When Kerk half-rose from his chair Jason stood too, shouting his words through the other man's fog of anger.

'I'm trying to help you – do you understand that? Wipe the hypocrisy out of your mind, it's destroying you. Right now you are fighting an already lost battle. This isn't a real war, just a disastrous treating of symptoms. Like cutting off cancerous fingers one by one. The only result must be ultimate defeat. You won't allow yourself to realize that. That's why you would rather kill me than hear me speak the unspeakable.'

Kerk was out of his seat now, hanging over Jason like a tower of death, about to fall. Held up only by the force of Jason's words.

'You must begin to face reality. All you can see is everlasting war. You must begin to realize that you can treat the *causes* of this war and end it forever!'

The meaning penetrated, the shock of the words draining away Kerk's anger. He dropped back into the chair, an almost ludicrous expression on his face. 'What the devil do you mean? You sound like a bloody grubber!'

Jason didn't ask what a grubber was, but he filed the name.

'You're talking nonsense,' Kerk said. 'This is just an alien world that must be battled. The causes are self-obvious facts of existence.'

'No, they're not,' Jason insisted. 'Consider for a second. When you are away for any length of time from this planet, you must take a refresher course. To see how things have changed for the worse while you were gone. Well, that's a linear progression. If things get worse when you extend into the future, then they have to get better if you extend into the past. It is also

55

good theory – though I don't know if the facts will bear me out – to say that if you extend it far enough into the past you will reach a time when mankind and Pyrrus were not at war with each other.'

Kerk was beyond speech now, only capable of sitting and listening while Jason drove home the blows of inescapable logic.

'There is evidence to support this theory. Even you will admit that I, if I am no match for Pyrran life, am surely well versed in it. And all Pyrran flora and fauna I've seen have one thing in common. They're not functional. *None* of their immense armoury of weapons is used against each other. Their toxins don't seem to operate against Pyrran life. They are good only for dispensing death to homo sapiens. And *that* is a physical impossibility. In the three hundred years that men have been on this planet, the life forms couldn't have naturally adapted in this manner.'

'But they *have* done it!' Kerk bellowed.

'You are so right,' Jason told him calmly. 'And if they have done it, there must be some agency at work. Operating how, I have no idea. But something has caused the life on Pyrrus to declare war, and I'd like to find out what that something is. What was the dominant life form here when your ancestors landed?'

'I'm sure I wouldn't know,' Kerk said. 'You're not suggesting, are you, that there are sentient beings on Pyrrus other than those of human descent? Creatures who are organizing the planet to battle us?'

'I'm not suggesting it – you are. That means you're getting the idea. I have no idea what caused this change, but I would sure like to find out. Then see if it can be changed back. Nothing promised, of course. You'll agree, though, that it is worth investigating.'

Fist smacking into his palm, his heavy footsteps shaking the building, Kerk paced back and forth the length of the room. He was at war with himself. New ideas fought old beliefs. It was so sudden – and so hard not to believe.

Without asking permission, Jason helped himself to some chilled water from the bottle and sank back into the chair, exhausted. Something whizzed in through the open window, tearing a hole in the protective screen. Kerk blasted it without changing stride, without even knowing he had done it.

The decision didn't take long. Geared to swift activity, the big Pyrran found it impossible not to decide quickly. The pacing stopped and he looked steadily at Jason.

'I don't say you have convinced me, but I find it impossible to find a ready answer to your arguments. So until I do, we will have to operate as if they are true. Now what do you plan to do, what *can* you do?'

Jason ticked the points off on his fingers. 'One, I'll need a place to live and work that is well protected. So instead of spending my energies on just remaining alive I can devote some study to his project. Two, I want someone to help me – and act as a bodyguard at the same time. And someone, please, with a little more scope of interest than my present watchdog. I would suggest Meta as the person most suited for this job.'

'Meta?' Kerk was surprised. 'She's a space pilot and defence screen operator; what good could she possibly be on a project like this?'

'The most good possible. She has had experience on other worlds and can shift her point of view – at least a bit. And she must know as much about this planet as any other educated adult and can answer any question I ask.' Jason smiled. 'In addition to which she is an attractive girl, whose company I enjoy.'

Kerk grunted. 'I was wondering if you would get around to mentioning that last reason. The others make sense, though, so I'm not going to argue. I'll round up a replacement for her and have Meta sent here. There are plenty of sealed buildings you can use.'

After talking to one of the assistants from the outer office, Kerk made some calls on the screen. The correct orders were quickly issued. Jason watched it all with interest.

'Pardon me for asking,' he finally said. 'But are you the dictator of this planet? You just snap your fingers and they all jump.'

'I suppose it looks that way,' Kerk admitted. 'But that is just an illusion. No one is in complete charge on Pyrrus, neither is

57

there anything resembling a democratic system. After all, our total population is about the size of an army division. Everyone does the job they are best qualified for. Various activities are separated into departments with the most qualified person in charge. I run Co-ordination and Supply, which is about the loosest category. We fill in the gaps between departments and handle procuring from off-planet.'

Meta came in then and talked to Kerk. She completely ignored Jason's presence. 'I was relieved and sent here,' she said. 'What is it? Change in flight schedule?'

'You might call it that,' Kerk said. 'As of now you are dismissed from all your old assignments and assigned to a new department, Investigation and Research. That tired-looking fellow there is your department head.'

'A sense of humour,' Jason said. 'The only native-born one on Pyrrus. Congratulations, there's hope for the planet yet.'

Meta glanced back and forth between them. 'I don't understand. I can't believe it. I mean a new department – why?' She was nervous and upset.

'I'm sorry,' Kerk said. 'I didn't mean to be cruel. I thought perhaps you might feel more at ease. What I said was true. Jason has a way – or may have a way – to be of immense value to Pyrrus. Will you help him?'

Meta had her composure back. And a little anger. 'Do I have to? Is that an order? You know I have work to do. I'm sure you will realize it is more important than something a person from *off-planet* might imagine. He can't really understand . . .'

'Yes. It's an order.' The snap was back in Kerk's voice. Meta flushed at the tone.

'Perhaps I can explain,' Jason broke in. 'After all, the whole thing is my idea. But first I would like your cooperation. Will you take the clip out of your gun and give it to Kerk?'

Meta looked frightened, but Kerk nodded in solemn agreement. 'Just for a few minutes, Meta. I have my gun so you will be safe here. I think I know what Jason has in mind, and from personal experience I'm afraid he is right.'

Reluctantly Meta passed over the clip and cleared the charge in the gun's chamber. Only then did Jason explain.

'I have a theory about life on Pyrrus, and I'm afraid I'll have to shatter some illusions when I explain. To begin with, the fact must be admitted that your people are slowly losing the war here and will eventually be destroyed. . . .'

Before he was half through the sentence, Meta's gun was directed between his eyes and she was wildly snapping the trigger. There was only hatred and revulsion in her expression. It was the most terrible thought in the world for her. That this war they all devoted their lives to was already lost.

Kerk took her by the shoulders and sat her in his chair, before anything worse happened. It took some time before she could calm down enough to listen to Jason's words. It is not easy to have destroyed the carefully built up rationalizations of a lifetime. Only the fact that she had seen something of other worlds enabled her to listen at all.

The light of unreason was still in her eyes when he had finished, telling her the things he and Kerk had discussed. She sat tensely, pushed forward against Kerk's hands, as if they were the only things that stopped her from leaping at Jason.

'Maybe that is too much to assimilate at one sitting,' Jason said. 'So let's put it in simpler terms. I believe we can find a reason for this unrelenting hatred of humans. Perhaps we don't smell right. Maybe I'll find an essence of crushed Pyrran bugs that will render us immune when we rub it in. I don't know yet. But whatever the results, we *must* make the investigation. Kerk agrees with me on that.'

Meta looked at Kerk and he nodded agreement. Her shoulders slumped in sudden defeat. She whispered the words.

'I – can't say I agree, or even understand all that you said. But I'll help you. If Kerk thinks that it is the right thing.'

'I do,' he said. 'Now, do you want the clip back for your gun? Not planning to take any more shots at Jason?'

'That was foolish of me,' she said coldly while she reloaded the gun. 'I don't need a gun. If I had to kill him, I could do it with my bare hands.'

'I love you too,' Jason smiled at her. 'Are you ready to go now?'

'Of course.' She brushed a fluffly curl of hair into place.

'First we'll find a place where you can stay. I'll take care of that. After that, the work of the new department is up to you.'

CHAPTER TEN

They walked downstairs in a frigid silence. In the street, Meta blasted a stingbird that couldn't possibly have attacked them. There was an angry pleasure in the act. Jason decided not to chide her about wasting ammo. Better the bird than him.

There were empty rooms in one of the computer buildings. These were completely sealed to keep stray animal life out of the delicate machinery. While Meta checked a bedroll out of stores, Jason painfully dragged a desk, table and chairs in from a near-by empty office. When she returned with a pneumatic bed, he instantly dropped on it with a grateful sigh. Her lip curled a bit at his obvious weakness.

'Get used to the sight,' he said. 'I intend to do as much of my work as I can while maintaining a horizontal position. You will be my strong right arm. And right now, Right Arm, I wish you could scare me up something to eat. I also intend to do most of my eating in the previously mentioned prone condition.'

Snorting with disgust, Meta stamped out. While she was gone, Jason chewed the end of a stylus thoughtfully, then made some careful notes.

After they had finished the almost tasteless meal, he began the search.

'Meta, where can I find historical records of Pyrrus? Any and all information about the early days of the settlers on this planet.'

'I've never heard of anything like that. I really don't know. . . .'

'But there has to be something – *somewhere*,' he insisted. 'Even if your present-day culture devotes all of its time and energies to survival, you can be sure it wasn't always that way. All the time it was developing, people were keeping records, making notes. Now where do we look? Do you have a library here?'

'Of course,' she said. 'We have an excellent technical library. But I'm sure there wouldn't be any of *that* sort of thing there.'

Trying not to groan, Jason stood up. 'Let me be the judge of that. Just lead the way.'

Operation of the library was completely automatic. A projected index gave the call number for any text that had to be consulted. The tape was delivered to the charge desk thirty seconds after the number had been punched. Returned tapes were dropped through a hopper and refiled automatically. The mechanism worked smoothly.

'Wonderful,' Jason said, pushing away from the index. 'A tribute to technological ingenuity. Only it contains nothing of any value to us. Just reams of textbooks.'

'What *else* should be in a library?' Meta sounded sincerely puzzled.

Jason started to explain, then changed his mind. 'Later we will go into that,' he said. 'Much later. Now we have to find a lead. Is it possible that there are any tapes – or even printed books – that aren't filed through this machine?'

'It seems unlikely, but we could ask Poli. He lives here somewhere and is in charge of the library. Filing new books and tending the machinery.'

The single door into the rear of the building was locked, and no amount of pounding could rouse the caretaker.

'If he's alive, this should do it,' Jason said. He pressed the out-of-order button on the control panel. It had the desired effect. Within five minutes, the door opened and Poli dragged himself through it.

Death usually came swiftly on Pyrrus. If wounds slowed a man down, the ever-ready forces of destruction quickly finished the job. Poli was the exception to this rule. Whatever had attacked him originally had done an efficient job. Most of the lower part of his face was gone. His left arm was curled and useless. The damage to his body and legs had left him with the bare capability to stumble from one spot to the next.

Yet he still had one good arm as well as his eyesight. He

61

could work in the library and relieve a fully fit man. How long he had been dragging the useless husk of a body around the building, no one knew. In spite of the pain that filled his red-rimmed, moist eyes, he had stayed alive. Growing old, older than any other Pyrran Jason had seen. He tottered forward and turned off the alarm that had called him.

When Jason started to explain, the old man took no notice. Only after the librarian had rummaged a hearing aid out of his clothes, did Jason realize he was deaf as well. Jason explained again what he searched for. Poli nodded and printed his answer on a tablet.

there are many books – in the store-rooms below.

Most of the building was taken up by the robot filing and sorting apparatus. They moved slowly through the banks of machinery, following the crippled librarian to a barred door in the rear. He pointed to it. While Jason and Meta fought to open the age-encrusted bars, he wrote another note on his tablet.

not opened for many years, rats.

Jason and Meta's guns appeared reflexively in their hands as they read the message. Jason finished opening the door by himself. The two native Pyrrans stood facing the opening gap. It was well they did. Jason could never have handled what came through that door.

He didn't even open it for himself. Their sounds at the door must have attracted all the vermin in the lower part of the building. Jason had thrown the last bolt and started to pull on the handle — when the door was *pushed* open from the other side.

Open the gateway to hell and see what comes out. Meta and Poli stood shoulder to shoulder firing into the mass of loath-someness that boiled through the door. Jason jumped to one side and picked off the occasional animal that came his way. The destruction seemed to go on for ever.

Long minutes passed before the last clawed beast made its death rush. Meta and Poli waited expectantly for more; they were happily excited by this chance to deal destruction. Jason felt a little sick after the silent ferocious attack. A ferocity that the Pyrrans reflected. He saw a scratch on Meta's face where one of the beasts had caught her. She seemed oblivious to it.

Pulling out his medikit, Jason circled the piled bodies. Something stirred in their midst and a crashing shot ploughed into it. Then he reached the girl and pushed the analyser probes against the scratch. The machine clicked and Meta jumped as the anti-toxin needle stabbed down. She realized for the first time what Jason was doing.

'Thank you, I didn't notice,' she said. 'There were so many of them and they came out so fast.'

Poli had a powerful battery lamp and, by unspoken agreement, Jason carried it. Crippled though he was, the old man was still a Pyrran when it came to handling a gun. They slowly made their way down the refuse-laden stairs.

'What a stench!' Jason grimaced. 'Without these filter plugs in my nose, I think the smell alone would kill me.'

Something hurled itself into the beam of light and a shot stopped it in mid-air. The rats had been there a long time and resented the intrusion.

At the foot of the stairs they looked around. There *had* been books and records there at one time. They had been systematically chewed, eaten and destroyed for decades.

'I like the care you take with your old books,' Jason said disgustedly. 'Remind me not to loan you any.'

'They could have been of no importance,' Meta said coolly, 'or they would be filed correctly in the library upstairs.'

Jason wandered gloomily through the rooms. Nothing remained of any value. Fragments and scraps of writing and printing. Never enough in one spot to bother collecting. With the toe of one armoured boot, he kicked angrily at a pile of debris, ready to give up the search. There was a glint of rusty metal under the dirt.

'Hold this!' He gave the light to Meta and, forgetting the danger for a moment, began scratching aside the rubble. A flat metal box with a dial lock built into it was revealed.

'Why, that's a log box!' Meta said, surprised.

'That's what I thought,' Jason said. 'And if it is – we may be in luck after all.'

CHAPTER ELEVEN

Resealing the cellar, they carried the box back to Jason's new office. Only after spraying with decontaminant did they examine it closely. Meta picked out engraved letters on the lid.

'S. T. POLLUX VICTORY – that must be the name of the spacer this log came from. But I don't recognize the class, or whatever it is the initials *S.T.* stand for.'

'Stellar Transport,' Jason told her, as he tried the lock mechanism. 'I've heard of them but I've never seen one. They were built during the last wave of galactic expansion. Really nothing more than gigantic metal containers, put together in space. After they were loaded with people, machinery and supplies, they would be towed to whatever planetary system had been chosen. These same tugs and one-shot rockets would brake the S.T.'s in for a landing. Then leave them there. The hull was a ready source of metal and the colonists could start right in building their new world. And they were *big*. All of them held at least fifty thousand people.'

Only after he said it, did he realize the significance of his words. Meta's deadly stare drove it home. There were now less people on Pyrrus than had been in the original settlement.

And human population, without rigid birth controls, usually increased geometrically. Jason remembered Meta's itchy trigger finger.

'But we can't be sure how many people were aboard this one,' he said hurriedly. 'Or even if this is the log of the ship that settled Pyrrus. Can you find something to pry this open with? The lock is corroded into a single lump.'

Meta took her anger out on the box. Her fingers managed to force a gap between lid and bottom. She wrenched at it. Rusty metal screeched and tore. The lid came off in her hands and a heavy book thudded to the table.

The cover legend destroyed all doubt.

Meta couldn't argue now. She stood behind Jason with tight-clenched fists and read over his shoulder as he turned the brittle, yellowed pages. He quickly skipped through the opening part that covered the sailing preparations and trip out. Only when he had reached the actual landing did he start reading slowly. The impact of the ancient words leaped out at him.

'Here it is!' Jason shouted. 'Proof positive that we're on the right trail. Even *you* will have to admit that. Read it, right here.'

. . . second day since the tugs left, we are completely on our own now. The settlers still haven't grown used to this planet, though we have orientation talks every night. As well as the morale agents whom I have working twenty hours a day. I suppose I really can't blame the people, they all lived in the underways of Setani and I doubt if they saw the sun once a year. This planet has weather with a vengeance, worse than anything I've seen on a hundred other planets. Was I wrong during the original planning stages not to insist on settlers from one of the agrarian worlds? People who could handle the outdoors. These citified Setanians are afraid to go out in the rain. But of course they have adapted completely to their native 1·5 gravity so the 2 gee here doesn't bother them much. That was the factor that decided us. Anyway, too late now to do anything about it. Or about the unending cycle of rain, snow, hail, hurricanes and such. Answer will be to start the mines going sell the metals and build completely enclosed cities.

The only thing on this forsaken planet that isn't actually against us are the animals. A few large predators at first, but the guards made short work of them. The rest of the wild life leaves us alone. Glad of that! They have been fighting for existence so long that I have never seen a more deadly looking collection. Even the little rodents no bigger than a man's hand are armoured like tanks. . . .

'I don't believe a word of it,' Meta broke in. 'That can't be Pyrrus he's writing about. . . .' Her words died away as Jason wordlessly pointed to the title on the cover.

He continued scanning the pages, flipping them quickly. A

sentence caught his eye and he stopped. Jamming his finger against the place, he read aloud.

'. . . and troubles keep piling up. First Har Palo with his theory that the volcanism is so close to the surface that the ground keeps warm, and the crops grow so well. Even if he is right – what can we do? We must be self-dependent if we intend to survive. And now this other thing. It seems that the forest fire drove a lot of new species our way. Animals, insects and even birds have attacked the people. (Note for Har: check if possible seasonal migration might explain attacks.) There have been fourteen deaths from wounds and poisoning. We'll have to enforce the rules for insect lotion at all times. And, I suppose, build some kind of perimeter defence to keep the larger beasts out of the camp.'

'This is a beginning,' Jason said. 'At least now we are aware of the real nature of the battle we're engaged in. It doesn't make Pyrrus any easier to handle, or make the life forms less dangerous, to know that they were once better disposed towards mankind. All this does is point the way. Something took the peaceful life forms, shook them up, and turned this planet into one big deathtrap for mankind. That *something* is what I want to uncover.'

CHAPTER TWELVE

Further reading of the log produced no new evidence. There was a good deal more information about the early animal and plant life and how deadly they were, as well as the first defences against them. Interesting historically, but of no use whatsoever in countering the menace. The captain apparently never thought that life forms were altering on Pyrrus, believing instead that dangerous beasts were being discovered. He never lived to change his mind. The last entry in the log, less than two months after the first attack, was very brief. And in a different handwriting.

Captain Kurkowski died today, of poisoning following an insect bite. His death is greatly mourned.

The 'why' of the planetary revulsion had yet to be uncovered.

'Kerk must see this book,' Jason said. 'He should have some idea of the progress being made. Can we get transportation – or do we walk to city hall?'

'Walk, of course,' Meta said.

'Then you bring the book. At two-G's I find it very hard to be a gentleman and carry the packages.'

They had just entered Kerk's outer office when a shrill screaming burst out of the phone screen. It took Jason a moment to realize that it was a mechanical signal, not a human voice.

'What is it?' he asked.

Kerk burst through the door and headed for the street entrance. Everyone else in the office was going the same way. Meta looked confused, leaning towards the door, then looking back at Jason.

'What does it mean? Can't you tell me?' He shook her arm.

'Sector alarm. A major break-through of some kind at the perimeter. Everyone but other perimeter guards has to answer.'

'Well, go then,' he said. 'Don't worry about me. I'll be all right.'

His words acted like a trigger release. Meta's gun was in her hand and she was gone before he had finished speaking. Jason sat down wearily in the deserted office.

The unnatural silence in the building began to get on his nerves. He shifted his chair over to the phone screen and switched it on to *receive*. The screen exploded with colour and sound. At first Jason could make no sense of it at all. Just a confused jumble of faces and voices. It was a multi-channel set designed for military use. A number of images were carried on the screen at one time, rows of heads or hazy backgrounds where the user had left the field of view. Many of the heads were talking at the same time and the babble of their voices made no sense whatsoever.

After examining the controls and making a few experiments, Jason began to understand the operation. Though all stations were on the screen at all times, their audio channels could be controlled. In that way two, three or more stations could be hooked together in a link-up. They would be in round-robin communication with each other, yet never out of contact with the other stations.

Identification between voice and sound was automatic. Whenever one of the pictured images spoke, the image would glow red. By trial and error, Jason brought in the audio for the stations he wanted and tried to follow the course of the attack.

Very quickly he realized this was something out of the ordinary. In some way, no one made it clear, a section of the perimeter had been broken through and emergency defences had to be thrown up to encapsulate it. Kerk seemed to be in charge, at least he was the only one with an over-ride transmitter. He used it for general commands. The many, tiny images faded and his face appeared on top of them, filling the entire screen.

'All perimeter stations send 25 per cent of your complement to Area 12.'

The small images reappeared and the babble increased, red lights flickering from face to face.

'— abandon the first floor, acid bombs can't reach.'

'If we hold we'll be cut off, but salient is past us on the west flank. Request support.'

'DON'T MERVV – IT'S USELESS!'

'. . . and the napalm tanks are almost gone. Orders?'

'The truck is still there, get it to the supply warehouse, you'll find replacements –'

Out of the welter of talk, only the last two fragments made any sense. Jason had noticed the signs below when he came in. The first two floors of the building below him were jammed with military supplies. This was his chance to get into the act.

Just sitting and watching was frustrating. Particularly when it was a desperate emergency. He didn't overvalue his worth, but he was sure there was always room for another gun.

By the time he had dragged himself down to the street level, a turbotruck had slammed to a stop in front of the loading platform. Two Pyrrans were rolling out drums of napalm with a reckless disregard for their own safety. Jason didn't dare enter that maelstrom of rolling metal. He found he could be of use tugging the heavy drums into position on the truck while the others rolled them up. They accepted his aid without acknow-ledgement.

It was exhausting, sweaty work, hauling the leaden drums into place against the heavy gravity. After a minute, Jason worked by touch through a red haze of hammering blood. He realized the job was done only when the truck suddenly leaped forward and he was thrown to the floor. He lay there, his chest heaving. As the driver hurled the heavy vehicle along, all Jason could do was bounce around on the bottom. He could see well enough, but was still gasping for breath when they braked at the fighting zone.

To Jason, it was a scene of incredible confusion. Guns firing, flames, men and women running on all sides. The napalm drums were unloaded without his help and the truck vanished for more. Jason leaned against a wall of a half-destroyed build-ing and tried to get his bearings. It was impossible. There seemed to be a great number of small animals; he killed two that attacked him. Other than that he couldn't determine the nature of the battle.

A Pyrran, tan face white with pain and exertion, stumbled up. His right arm, wet with raw flesh and dripping blood, hung limply at his side. It was covered with freshly applied surgical foam. He held his gun in his left hand, a stump of control cable dangling from it. Jason thought the man was looking for medi-cal aid. He couldn't have been more wrong.

Clenching the gun in his teeth, the Pyrran clutched a barrel of napalm with his good hand and hurled it over on its side. Then, with the gun once more in his hand, he began to roll the drum along the ground with his feet. It was slow, cumbersome work, but he was still in the fight.

Jason pushed through the hurrying crowd and bent over the drum. 'Let me do it,' he said. 'You can cover us both with your gun.'

The man wiped the sweat from his eyes with the back of his arm and blinked at Jason. He seemed to recognize him. When he smiled it was a grimace of pain, empty of humour. 'Do that. I can still shoot. Two half men – maybe we equal one whole.' Jason was labouring too hard to even notice the insult.

An explosion had blasted a raw pit in the street ahead. Two

people were at the bottom, digging it even deeper with shovels. The whole thing seemed meaningless. Just as Jason and the wounded man rolled up the drum, the diggers leaped out of the excavation and began shooting down into its depths. One of them turned, a young girl, barely in her teens.

'Praise Perimeter!' she breathed. 'They found the napalm. One of the new horrors is breaking through towards Area 13, we just found it.' Even as she talked she swivelled the drum around, kicked the easy-off plug, and began dumping the gelid contents into the hole. When half of it had gurgled down, she kicked the drum itself in. Her companion pulled a flare from his belt, lit it, and threw it after the drum.

'Back quick. They don't like heat,' he said.

This was putting it very mildly. The napalm caught, tongues of flame and rolling, greasy smoke climbing up to the sky. Under Jason's feet the earth shifted and moved. *Something* black and long stirred in the heart of the flame, then arched up into the sky over their heads. In the midst of the searing heat, it still moved with alien, jolting motions. It was immense, at least two metres thick and with no indication of its length. The flames didn't stop it, just annoyed it.

Jason had some idea of the thing's length as the street cracked and buckled for fifty metres on each side of the pit. Great loops of the creature began to emerge from the ground. He fired his gun, as did the others. Not that it seemed to have any effect. More and more people were appearing, armed with a variety of weapons. Flamethrowers and grenades seemed to be the most effective.

Clear the area, we're going to saturate it. Fall back.

The voice was so loud it jarred Jason's ear. He turned and recognized Kerk, who had arrived with truckloads of equipment. He had a power speaker on his back, the mike hung in front of his lips. His amplified voice brought an instant reaction from the crowd. They began to move.

There was still doubt in Jason's mind what to do. Clear the area? But what area? He started towards Kerk, before he realized that the rest of the Pyrrans were going in the opposite direction. Even under two gravities, they *moved*.

Jason had a naked feeling of being alone on the stage. He

was in the centre of the street, and the others had vanished. No one remained. Except the wounded man Jason had helped. He stumbled towards Jason, waving his good arm. Jason couldn't understand what he said. Kerk was shouting orders again from one of the trucks. They had started to move too. The urgency struck home and Jason started to run.

It was too late. On all sides the earth was buckling, cracking, as more loops of the underground thing forced its way into the light. Safety lay ahead. Only in front of it rose an arch of dirt-encrusted grey.

There are seconds of time that seem to last an eternity. A moment of subjective time that is grabbed and stretched to an infinite distance. This was one of those moments. Jason stood, frozen. Even the smoke in the sky hung unmoving. The high-standing loop of alien life was before him, every detail piercingly clear.

Thick as a man, ribbed and grey as old bark. Tendrils projected from all parts of it, pallid and twisting lengths that writhed slowly with snake-like life. Shaped like a plant, yet with the motions of an animal. And cracking, splitting. This was the worst.

Seams and openings appeared. Splintering, gaping mouths that vomited out a horde of pallid animals. Jason heard their shriekings, shrill yet remote. He saw the needle-like teeth that lined their jaws.

The paralysis of the unknown held him there. He should have died. Kerk was thundering at him through the power speaker, others were firing into the attacking creature. Jason knew nothing.

Then he shot forward, pushed by a rock-hard shoulder. The wounded man was still there, trying to get Jason clear. Gun clenched in his jaws, he dragged Jason along with his good arm. Towards the creature. The others stopped firing. They saw his plan and it was a good one.

A loop of the thing arched into the air, leaving an opening between its body and the ground. The wounded Pyrran planted his feet and tightened his muscles. One-handed, with a single thrust, he picked Jason off the ground and sent him hurtling under the living arch. Moving tendrils brushed fire along his face, then he was through, rolling over and over on the ground. The wounded Pyrran leaped after him.

It was too late. There had been a chance for one person to get out. The Pyrran could have done it easily – instead he had pushed Jason first. The thing was aware of movement when Jason brushed its tendrils. It dropped and caught the wounded man under its weight. He vanished from sight as the tendrils wrapped around him and the animals swarmed over. His trigger must have pulled back to full automatic because the gun kept firing a long time after he should have been dead.

Jason crawled. Some of the fanged animals ran towards him, but were shot. He knew nothing about this. Then rude hands grabbed him up and pulled him forward. He slammed into the side of a truck and Kerk's face was in front of his, flushed and angry. One of the giant fists closed on the front of Jason's clothes and he was lifted off his feet, shaken like a limp bag of rags. He offered no protest and could not have even if Kerk had killed him.

When he was thrown to the ground, someone picked him up and slid him into the back of the truck. He did not lose consciousness as the truck bounced away, yet he could not move. In a moment the fatigue would go away and he would sit up. That was all he was, just a little tired. Even as he thought this, he passed out.

CHAPTER THIRTEEN

'Just like old times,' Jason said when Brucco came into the room with a tray of food. Without a word Brucco served Jason and the wounded men in the other beds, then left. 'Thanks,' Jason called after his retreating back.

A joke, a twist of a grin, like it always was. Sure. But even as he grinned and his lips shaped a joke, Jason felt them like a veneer on the outside. Something plastered on with a life of its own. Inside he was numb and immovable. His body was stiff as his eyes still watched that arch of alien flesh descend and smother the one-armed Pyrran with its million burning fingers.

He could feel himself under the arch. After all, hadn't the

72

wounded man taken his place? He finished the meal without realizing that he ate.

Ever since that morning, when he had recovered consciousness, it had been like this. He knew that he should have died out there in that battle-torn street. *His* life should have been snuffed out, for making the mistake of thinking that he could actually help the battling Pyrrans. Instead of being underfoot and in the way. If it hadn't been for Jason, the man with the wounded arm would have been brought here to the safety of the reorientation buildings. He knew he was lying in the bed that belonged to that man.

The man who had given his life for Jason's.

The man whose name he didn't even know.

There were drugs in the food and they made him sleep. The medicated pads soaked the pain and rawness out of the burns where the tentacles had seared his face. When he awoke the second time, his touch with reality had been restored.

A man had died so he could live. Jason faced the fact. He couldn't restore that life, no matter how much he wanted to. What he could do was make the man's death worthwhile. If it can be said that any death was worthwhile. . . . He forced his thoughts from that track.

Jason knew what he had to do. His work was even more important now. If he could solve the riddle of this deadly world, he could repay in part the debt he owed.

Sitting up made his head spin and he held to the edge of the bed until it slowed down. The others in the room ignored him as he slowly and painfully dragged on his clothes. Brucco came in, saw what he was doing, and left again without a word.

Dressing took a long time, but it was finally done. When Jason finally left the room he found Kerk waiting there for him.

'Kerk, I want to tell you. . . .'

'Tell me *nothing*!' The thunder of Kerk's voice bounced back from the ceiling and walls. 'I'm telling *you*. I'll tell you once and that will be the end of it. You're not wanted on Pyrrus, Jason dinAlt, neither you nor your precious off-world schemes are wanted here. I let you convince me once with your twisted tongue. Helped you at the expense of more important work. I should have known what the result of your "logic"

73

would be. Now I've seen. Welf died so you could live. He was twice the man you will ever be.'

'Welf? Was that his name?' Jason asked stumblingly. 'I didn't know. . . .'

'You didn't even know.' Kerk's lips pulled back from his teeth in a grimace of disgust. 'You didn't even know his name – yet he died that you might continue your miserable existence.' Kerk spat, as if the words gave a vile flavour to his speech, and stamped towards the exit lock. Almost as an afterthought, he turned back to Jason.

'You'll stay here in the sealed buildings until the ship returns in two weeks. Then you will leave this planet and never come back. If you do I'll kill you instantly. With pleasure.' He started through the lock.

'Wait,' Jason shouted. 'You can't decide like that. You haven't even seen the evidence I've uncovered. Ask Meta –' The lock thumped shut and Kerk was gone.

The whole thing was just too stupid. Anger began to replace the futile despair of a moment before. He was being treated like an irresponsible child, the importance of his discovery of the log completely ignored.

Jason turned and saw for the first time that Brucco was standing there. 'Did you hear that?' Jason asked him.

'Yes. And I quite agree. You can consider yourself lucky.'

'Lucky!' Jason was the angry one now. 'Lucky to be treated like a moronic child, with contempt for everything I do –'

'I said lucky,' Brucco snapped. 'Welf was Kerk's only surviving son. Kerk had high hopes for him, was training him to take his place eventually.' He turned to leave but Jason called after him.

'Wait. I'm sorry about Welf. I can't be any sorrier knowing that he was Kerk's son. But at least it explains why Kerk is so quick to throw me out – as well as the evidence I have uncovered. The log of the ship . . .'

'I know, I've seen it,' Brucco interrupted.' Meta brought it in. Very interesting historical document.'

'That's all you can see it as, a historical document? The significance of the planetary change escapes you?'

'It doesn't escape me,' Brucco answered briefly. 'But I cannot see that it has any relevancy today. The past is unchangeable and we must fight in the present. That is enough to occupy all our energies.'

The pressure of futility built up inside Jason, fighting for a way to burst free. Wherever he turned, there was only indifference.

'You're an intelligent man, Brucco – yet you can see no further than the tip of your own nose. I suppose it is inevitable. You and the rest of the Pyrrans are supermen by Earth standards. Tough, ruthless, unbeatable, fast on the draw. Drop you anywhere and you land on your feet. You would make perfect Texas Rangers, Canadian Mounties, Venus Swamp Patrolmen – any of the mythical frontier fighters of the past. And I think that's where you really belong. In the past. On Pyrrus, mankind has been pushed to the limit of adaptability in muscle and reflex. And it's a dead end. Brain was the thing that dragged mankind out of the caves and started him on his way to the stars. When we start thinking with our muscles again we are on our way right back to those caves. Isn't that what you Pyrrans are? A bunch of cavemen hitting animals on the head with stone axes. Do you ever stop to think why you are here? What you are doing? Where you are going?'

Jason had to stop; he was exhausted and gasping for breath. Brucco rubbed his chin in thought. 'Caves?' he asked. 'Of course we don't live in caves or use stone clubs. I don't understand your point at all.'

It was impossible to be angry, or even exasperated. Jason started to answer, then laughed instead. A very humourless laugh. He was too tired to argue any more. He kept running into this same stone wall with all the Pyrrans. Theirs was a logic of the moment. The past and future unchangeable, unknowable – and uninteresting. 'How is the perimeter battle going?' he asked finally, wanting to change the subject.

'Finished. Or in the last stages at least.' Brucco was enthusiastic as he showed Jason stereos of the attackers. He did not notice Jason's repressed shudder.

'This was the most serious break-through in years, but we caught it in time. I hate to think what would have happened if they hadn't been detected for a few weeks more.'

'What are those things?' Jason asked. 'Giant snakes of some kind?'

'Don't be absurd,' Brucco snorted. He tapped the stereo with his thumbnail. 'Roots. That's all. Greatly modified, but still roots. They came in under the perimeter barrier, much deeper than anything we've had before. Not a real threat in themselves as they have very little mobility. Die soon after being cut. The danger came from their being used as access tunnels. They're bored through and through with animal runs, and two or three species of beasts live in a sort of symbiosis inside. Now we know what they are we can watch for them. The danger was they could have completely undermined the perimeter and come in from all sides at once. Not much we could have done then.'

The edge of destruction. Living on the lip of a volcano. The Pyrrans took satisfaction from any day that passed without total annihilation. There seemed no way to change their attitude. Jason let the conversation die there. He picked up the log of the *Pollux Victory* from Brucco's quarters, and carried it back to his room. The wounded Pyrrans there ignored him as he dropped on to the bed and opened the book to the first page.

For two days he did not leave his quarters. The wounded men were soon gone and he had the room to himself. Page by page he went through the log, until he knew every detail of the settlement of Pyrrus. His notes and cross-references piled up. He made an accurate map of the original settlement, superimposed over a modern one. They didn't match at all.

It was a dead end. With one map held over the other, what he had suspected was painfully clear. The descriptions of terrain and physical features in the log were accurate enough. The city had obviously been moved since the first landing. Whatever records had been kept would be in the library – and he had exhausted that source. Anything else would have been left behind and long since destroyed.

Rain lashed against the thick window above his head, lit suddenly by a flare of lightning. The unseen volcanoes were active again, vibrating the floor with their rumblings deep in the earth.

The shadow of defeat pressed heavily down on Jason. Rounding his shoulders and darkening, even more, the overcast day.

CHAPTER FOURTEEN

Jason spent one depressed day lying on his bunk counting rivets, forcing himself to accept defeat. Kerk's order that he was not to leave the sealed building tied his hands completely. He felt himself close to the answer – but he was never going to get it.

One day of defeat was all he could take. Kerk's attitude was completely emotional, untempered by the slightest touch of logic. This fact kept driving home until Jason could no longer ignore it. Emotional reasoning was something he had learned to mistrust early in life. He couldn't agree with Kerk in the slightest – which meant he had to utilize the ten remaining days to solve the problem. If it meant disobeying Kerk, it would still have to be done.

He grabbed up his noteplate with a new enthusiasm. His first sources of information had been used up, but there must be others. Chewing the scriber and thinking hard, he slowly built up a list of other possibilities. Any idea, no matter how wild, was put down. When the plate was filled, he wiped off the long shots and impossibles – such as consulting off-world historical records. This was a Pyrran problem and had to be settled on this planet or not at all.

The list worked down to two probables. Either old records, notebooks or diaries that individual Pyrrans might have in their possession, or verbal histories that had been passed down the generations by word of mouth. The first choice seemed to be the most probable and he acted on it at once. After a careful check of his medikit and gun, he went to see Brucco.

'What's new and deadly in the world since I left?' he asked.

Brucco glared at him. 'You can't go out, Kerk has forbidden it.'

'Did he put you in charge of guarding me to see if I obeyed?' Jason's voice was quiet and cold.

77

Brucco rubbed his jaw and frowned in thought. Finally he just shrugged. 'No, I'm not guarding you – nor do I want the job. As far as I know, this is between you and Kerk and it can stay that way. Leave whenever you want. And get yourself killed quietly some place so there will be an end to the trouble you cause once and for all.'

'I like you too,' Jason said. 'Now brief me on the wild-life.'

The only new mutation that routine precautions wouldn't take care of was a slate-coloured lizard that spit a fast nerve poison with deadly accuracy. Death took place in seconds if the saliva touched any bare skin. The lizards had to be looked out for, and shot before they came within range. An hour of lizard-blasting in a training chamber made him proficient in the exact procedure.

Jason left the sealed buildings quietly and no one saw him go. He followed the map to the nearest barracks, shuffling tiredly through the dusty streets. It was a hot, quiet afternoon, broken only by rumblings from the distance, and the occasional crack of his gun.

It was cool inside the thick-walled barracks building, and he collapsed on to a bench until the sweat dried and his heart stopped pounding. Then he went to the nearest recreation room to start his search.

Before it began, it was finished. None of the Pyrrans kept old artifacts of any kind and thought the whole idea was very funny. After the twentieth negative answer, Jason was ready to admit defeat in this line of investigation. There was as much chance of meeting a Pyrran with old documents as finding a bundle of Grandfather's letters in a soldier's kit bag.

This left a single possibility – verbal histories. Again Jason questioned with the same lack of results. The fun had worn off the game for the Pyrrans and they were beginning to growl. Jason stopped while he was still in one piece. The commissary served him a meal that tasted like plastic paste and wood pulp. He ate it quickly, then sat brooding over the empty tray, hating to admit to another dead end. Who could supply him with answers? All the people he had talked to were so young. They had no interest or patience for story-telling. That was an old folks' hobby – and there were no oldsters on Pyrrus.

With one exception that he knew of, the librarian, Poli. It was a possibility. A man who worked with records and books might have an interest in some of the older ones. He might even remember reading volumes now destroyed. A very slim lead, indeed, but one that had to be pursued.

Walking to the library almost killed Jason. The torrential rains made the footing bad, and in the dim light it was hard to see what was coming. A snapper came in close enough to take out a chunk of flesh before he could blast it. The antitoxin made him dizzy and he lost some blood before he could get the wound dressed. He reached the library, exhausted and angry.

Poli was working on the guts of one of the catalogue machines. He didn't stop until Jason had tapped him on the shoulder. Switching on his hearing aid, the Pyrran stood quietly, crippled and bent, waiting for Jason to talk.

'Have you any old papers or letters that you have kept for your personal use?'

A shake of the head, *no*.

'What about stories – you know, about great things that have happened in the past, that someone might have told you when you were young?' Negative.

Results negative. Every question was answered by a shake of Poli's head, and very soon the old man grew irritated and pointed to the work he hadn't finished.

'Yes, I know you have work to do,' Jason said. 'But this is important.' Poli shook his head an angry *no* and reached to turn off his hearing aid. Jason groped for a question that might get a more positive answer. There was something tugging at his mind, a word he had heard and made a note of, to be investigated later. Something that Kerk had said. . . .

'That's it!' It was right there – on the tip of his tongue. 'Just a second, Poli, just one more question. What is a "grubber"?' Have you ever seen one or do you know what they do, or where they can be found?'

The words were cut off as Poli whirled and lashed the back of his good arm into Jason's face. Though the man was aged and crippled, the blow almost fractured Jason's jaw, sending him sliding across the floor. Through a daze, he saw Poli hobbling towards him, making thick bubbling noises in his ruined

79

throat, what remained of his face twisted and working with anger.

This was no time for diplomacy. Moving as fast as he could, with the high-G, foot-slapping shuffle, Jason headed for the sealed door. He was no match for any Pyrran in hand-to-hand combat, young and small or old and crippled. The door banged open as he went through, and barely closed in Poli's face.

Outside the rain had turned to snow and Jason trudged wearily through the slush, rubbing his sore jaw and turning over the only fact he had. *Grubber* was a key – but to what? And who did he dare ask for more information? Kerk was the man he had talked to best, but not any more. That left only Meta as a possible source. He wanted to see her at once, but sudden exhaustion swept through him. It took all of his strength to stumble back to the school buildings.

In the morning he ate and left early. There was only a week left. It was impossible to hurry and he cursed as he dragged his double-weight body to the assignment centre. Meta was on night perimeter duty and should be back to her quarters soon. He shuffled over there and was lying on her bunk when she came in.

'Get out,' she said in a flat voice. 'Or do I throw you out?'

'Patience, please,' he said as he sat up. 'Just resting here until you came back. I have a single question, and if you will answer it for me I'll go and stop bothering you.'

'What is it?' she asked, tapping her foot with impatience. But there was also a touch of curiosity in her voice. Jason thought carefully before he spoke.

'Now try not to shoot me. You know I'm an off-worlder with a big mouth, and you have heard me say some awful things without taking a shot at me. Now I have another one. Will you please show your superiority to the other people of the galaxy by holding your temper and not reducing me to component atoms.'

Her only answer was a tap of the foot, so he took a deep breath and plunged in.

'What is a "grubber"?'.

For a long moment she was quiet, unmoving. Then she

looked at him with disgust. 'You do find the most repulsive topics.'

'That may be,' he said, 'but it still doesn't answer my question.'

'It's . . . well, the sort of thing people just don't talk about.'

'I do,' he assured her.

'Well I *don't*! It's the most disgusting thing in the world, and that's all I'm going to say. Talk to Krannon, but not to me.' She had him by the arm while she talked and he was half dragged to the hall. The door slammed behind him and he muttered '*Lady-wrestler*' under his voice. His anger ebbed away as he realized that she had given him a clue in spite of herself. Next step, find out who or what Krannon was.

Assignment centre listed a man named Krannon and gave his shift number and work location. It was close by and Jason walked there. A large, cubical, windowless building, with the single word FOOD next to each of the sealed entrances. The small entrance he went through was a series of automatic chambers that cycled him through ultrasonics, ultraviolet, anti-bio spray, rotating brushes and three final rinses. He was finally admitted, damper but much cleaner, to the central area. Men and robots were stacking crates and he asked one of the men for Krannon. The man looked him up and down coldly and spat on his shoes before answering.

Krannon worked in a large storage bay by himself. He was a stocky man in patched coveralls whose only expression was one of intense gloom. When Jason came in he stopped hauling bales and sat down on the nearest one. The lines of unhappiness were cut into his face and seemed to grow deeper while Jason explained what he was after. All the talk of ancient history on Pyrrus bored him as well and he yawned openly. When Jason finished, he yawned again and didn't even bother to answer him.

Jason waited a moment, then asked again. 'I said do you have any old books, papers, records or that sort of thing?'

'You sure picked the right guy to bother, off-worlder,' was his only answer. 'After talking to me you're going to have nothing but trouble.'

'Why is that?' Jason asked.

'Why?' For the first time, he was animated with something besides grief. 'I'll tell you why! I made one mistake once, just one, and I get a life sentence. For life – how would you like that. Just me alone, being by myself all the time. Even taking orders from the grubbers.'

Jason controlled himself, keeping the elation out of his voice. 'Grubbers? What are grubbers?'

The enormity of the question stopped Krannon; it seemed impossible that there could be a man alive who had never heard of grubbers. Happiness lifted some of the gloom from his face as he realized that he had a captive audience who would listen to his troubles.

'Grubbers are traitors – that's what they are. Traitors to the human race and they ought to be wiped out. Living in the jungle. The things they do with the animals. . . .'

'You mean they're people – Pyrrans like yourself?' Jason broke in.

'Not like *me*, mister. Don't make that mistake again if you want to go on living. Maybe I dozed off on guard once so I got stuck with this job. That doesn't mean I like it or like them. They stink, really stink, and if it wasn't for the food we get from them they'd all be dead tomorrow. That's the kind of killing job I could really put my heart into.'

'If they supply you with food, you must give them something in return?'

'Trade goods, beads, knives, the usual things. Supply sends them over in cartons and I take care of the delivery.'

'How?' Jason asked.

'By armoured truck to the delivery site. Then I go back later to pick up the food they've left in exchange.'

'Can I go with you on the next delivery?'

Krannon frowned over the idea for a minute. 'Yeah, I suppose it's all right if you're stupid enough to come. You can help me load. They're between harvests now, so the next trip won't be for eight days. . . .'

'But that's after the ship leaves – it'll be too late. Can't you go earlier?'

'Don't tell me your troubles, mister,' Krannon grumbled, climbing to his feet. 'That's when I go and the date's not changing for you.'

Jason realized he had got as much out of the man as was possible for one session. He started for the door, then turned.

'One thing,' he asked. 'Just what do these savages – the grubbers – look like?'

'How do I know!' Krannon snapped. 'I trade with them, I don't make love to them. If I ever saw one, I'd shoot him down on the spot.' He flexed his fingers and his gun jumped in and out of his hand as he said it. Jason quietly let himself out.

Lying on his bunk, resting his gravity-weary body, he searched for a way to get Krannon to change the delivery date. His millions of credits were worthless on this world without currency. If the man couldn't be convinced, he had to be bribed. With what? Jason's eyes touched the locker where his off-world clothing still hung, and he had an idea.

It was morning before he could return to the food warehouse – and one day closer to his deadline. Krannon didn't bother to look up from his work when Jason came in.

'Do you want this?' Jason said, handing the outcast a flat, gold case inset with a single large diamond. Krannon grunted and turned it over in his hands.

'A toy,' he said. 'What is it good for?'

'Well, when you press this button you get a light.' A flame appeared through a hole in the top. Krannon started to hand it back.

'What do I need a little fire for? Here, keep it.'

'Wait a second,' Jason said. 'That's not all it does. When you press the jewel in the centre, one of these comes out.' A black pellet the size of his fingernail dropped into his palm. 'A grenade, made of solid ultranite. Just squeeze it hard and throw. Three seconds later it explodes with enough force to blast open this building.'

This time Krannon almost smiled as he reached for the case. Destructive and death-dealing weapons are like candy to a Pyrran. While he looked at it, Jason made his offer.

'The case and bombs are yours if you move the date of your

83

next delivery up to tomorrow – and let me go with you.'

'Be here at 05.00,' Krannon said. 'We leave early.'

CHAPTER–FIFTEEN

The truck rumbled up to the perimeter gate and stopped. Krannon waved to the guards through the front window, then closed a metal shield over it. When the gates swung open the truck – really a giant armoured tank – ground slowly forward. There was a second gate beyond the first, that did not open until the interior one was closed. Jason looked through the second driver's periscope as the outer gate lifted. Automatic flamethrowers flared through the opening, cutting off only when the truck reached them. A scorched area ringed the gate; beyond that the jungle began. Unconsciously Jason shrank back in his seat.

All the plants and animals he had seen only specimens of existed here in profusion. Thorn-ringed branches and vines laced themselves into a solid mat, through which the wild life swarmed. A fury of sound hurled at them, thuds and scratchings rang on the armour. Krannon laughed and closed the switch that electrified the outer grid. The scratchings died away as the beast completed the circuit to the grounded hull.

It was slow-speed, low-gear work tearing through the jungle. Krannon had his face buried in the periscope mask and silently fought the controls. With each mile, the going seemed to get better, until he finally swung up the periscope and opened the window armour. The jungle was still thick and deadly, but nothing like the area immediately around the perimeter. It appeared as if most of the lethal powers of Pyrrus were concentrated in the single area around the settlement. Why? Jason asked himself. Why this intense and directed planetary hatred?

The motors died and Krannon stood up, stretching. 'We're here,' he said. 'Let's unload.'

There was bare rock around the truck, a rounded hillock that projected from the jungle, too smooth and steep for vegetation to get a hold. Krannon opened the cargo hatches and they

84

pushed out the boxes and crates. When they finished Jason slumped down, exhausted, on to the pile.

'Get back in, we're leaving,' Krannon said.

'You are, I'm staying right here.'

Krannon looked at him coldly. 'Get in the truck or I'll kill you. No one stays out here. For one thing you couldn't live an hour alone. But worse than that the grubbers would get you. Kill you at once, of course, but that's not important. But you have equipment that we can't allow into their hands. You want to see a grubber with a gun?'

While the Pyrran talked, Jason's thoughts had rushed ahead. He hoped that Krannon was as thick of head as he was fast of reflex.

Jason looked at the trees, let his gaze move up through the thick branches. Though Krannon was still talking, he was automatically aware of Jason's attention. When Jason's eyes widened and his gun jumped into his hand, Krannon's own gun appeared and he turned in the same direction.

'There – in the top!' Jason shouted and fired into the tangle of branches. Krannon fired too. As soon as he did, Jason hurled himself backwards, curled into a ball, rolling down the inclined rock. The shots had covered the sounds of his movements, and before Krannon could turn back the gravity had dragged him down the rock into the thick foliage. Crashing branches slapped at him, but slowed his fall. When he stopped moving, he was lost in the tangle. Krannon's shots came too late to hit him.

Lying there, tired and bruised, Jason heard the Pyrran cursing him. He stamped around on the rock, fired a few shots, but knew better than to enter the trees. Finally he gave up and went back to the truck. The motor gunned into life and the treads clanked and scraped down the rock and back into the jungle. There were muted rumblings and crashes that slowly died away.

Then Jason was alone.

Up until that instant he hadn't realized quite how alone he would be. Surrounded by nothing but death, the truck already vanished from sight. He had to force down an overwhelming desire to run after it. What was done was done.

This was a long chance to take, but it was the only way to contact the grubbers. They were savages, but still they had come from human stock. And they hadn't sunk so low as to stop the barter with the civilized Pyrrans. He had to contact them, befriend them. Find out how they had managed to live safely in this madhouse world.

If there had been another way to lick the problem he would have taken it; he didn't relish the role of martyred hero. But Kerk and his deadline had forced his hand. The contact had to be made fast and this was the only way.

There was no telling where the savages were, or how soon they would arrive. If the woods weren't too lethal, he could hide there, pick his time to approach them. If they found him among the supplies, they might skewer him on the spot with a typical Pyrran reflex.

Walking warily, he approached the line of trees. Something moved on a branch, but vanished as he came near. None of the plants near a thick-trunked tree looked poisonous, so he slipped behind it. There was nothing deadly in sight and it surprised him. He let his body relax a bit, leaning against the rough bark.

Something soft and choking fell over his head; his body was seized in a steel grip. The more he struggled, the tighter it held him until the blood thundered in his ears and his lungs screamed for air.

Only when he grew limp did the pressure let up. His first panic ebbed a little when he realized that it wasn't an animal that attacked him. He knew nothing about the grubbers, but they were human, so he still had a chance.

His arms and legs were tied, the power holster ripped from his arm. He felt strangely naked without it. The powerful hands grabbed him again and he was hurled into the air, to fall face down across something warm and soft. Fear pressed in again for it was a large animal of some kind. And all Pyrran animals were deadly.

When the animal moved off, carrying him, panic was replaced by a feeling of mounting elation. The grubbers had managed to work out a truce of some kind with at least one form of animal life. He had to find out how. If he could get that secret – and get it back to the city – it would justify all his work and pain. It might even justify Welf's death if the age-old war could be slowed or stopped.

Jason's tightly bound limbs hurt terribly at first, but grew numb with the circulation shut off. The jolting ride continued endlessly; he had no way of measuring the time. A rainfall soaked him, then he felt his clothes steaming as the sun came out.

The ride was finally over. He was pulled from the animal's back and dumped down. His arms dropped free as someone loosed the bindings. The returning circulation soaked him in pain as he lay there, struggling to move. When his hands finally obeyed him, he lifted them to his face and stripped away the covering, a sack of thick fur. Light blinded him as he sucked in breath after breath of clean air.

Blinking against the glare, he looked around. He was lying on a floor of crude planking, the setting sun shining into his eyes through the doorless entrance of the building. There was a ploughed field outside, stretching down the curve of hill to the edge of the jungle. It was too dark to see much inside the hut.

Something blocked the light of the doorway, a tall animal-like figure. On second look Jason realized it was a man with long hair and thick beard. He was dressed in furs; even his legs were wrapped in fur leggings. His eyes were fixed on his captive, while one hand fondled an axe that hung from his waist.

'Who're you? What y'want?' the bearded man asked suddenly.

Jason picked his words slowly, wondering if this savage had the same hair-trigger temper as the city dwellers.

'My name is Jason. I come in peace. I want to be your friend. . . .'

'Lies!' the man grunted, and pulled the axe from his belt. 'Junkman tricks. I saw y'hide. Wait to kill me. Kill you first.' He tested the edge of the blade with a horny thumb, then raised it.

'Wait!' Jason said desperately. 'You don't understand.'

The axe swung down.

'I'm from off-world and –'

A solid thunk shook him as the axe buried itself in the wood

87

next to his head. At the last instant, the man had twitched it aside. He grabbed the front of Jason's clothes and pulled him up until their faces touched.

'S'true?' he shouted. 'Y'from off-world?' His hand opened and Jason dropped back before he could answer. The savage jumped over him, towards the dim rear of the hut.

'Rhes must know of this,' he said as he fumbled with something in the wall. Light sprang out.

All Jason could do was stare. The hairy, fur-covered savage was operating a communicator. The calloused, dirt-encrusted fingers deftly snapped open the circuits, dialled a number.

CHAPTER–SIXTEEN

It made no sense. Jason tried to reconcile the modern machine with the barbarian and couldn't. Who was he calling? The existence of one communicator meant there was at least another. Was Rhes a person or a thing?

With a mental effort, he grabbed hold of his thoughts and braked them to a stop. There was something new here, factors he hadn't counted on. He kept reassuring himself there was an explanation for everything, once you had your facts straight.

Jason closed his eyes, shutting out the glaring rays of the sun where it cut through the tree-tops, and reconsidered his facts. They separated evenly into two classes: those he had observed for himself, and those he had learned from the city dwellers. This last class of 'facts' he would hold, to see if they fitted with what he learned. There was a good chance that most, or all, of them would prove false.

'Get up,' the voice jarred into his thoughts. 'We're leaving.'

His legs were still numb and hardly usable. The bearded man snorted in disgust and hauled him to his feet, propping him against the outer wall. Jason clutched the knobby bark of the logs when he was left alone. He looked around, soaking up impressions.

It was the first time he had been on a farm since he had run away from home. A different world with a different ecology, but the similarity was apparent enough to him. A new-sown field stretched down the hill in front of the shack. Ploughed by a good farmer. Even, well-cast furrows that followed the contour of the slope. Another, larger log building was next to this one, probably a barn.

There was a snuffing sound behind him and Jason turned quickly – and froze. His hand called for the missing gun and his finger tightened down on a trigger that wasn't there.

It had come out of the jungle and padded up quietly behind him. It had six thick legs with clawed feet that dug into the ground. The two-metre-long body was covered with matted yellow-and-black fur, all except the skull and shoulders. These were covered with overlapping horny plates. Jason could see all this because the beast was that close.

He waited to die.

The mouth opened, a frog-like division of the hairless skull, revealing double rows of jagged teeth.

'Here, Fido,' the bearded man said, coming up behind Jason and snapping his fingers at the same time. The thing bounded forward, brushing past the dazed Jason, and rubbed his head against the man's leg. 'Nice doggie,' the man said, his fingers scratching under the edge of the carapace where it joined the flesh.

The bearded man had brought two of the riding animals out of the barn, saddled and bridled. Jason barely noticed the details of smooth skin and long legs, as he swung up on one. His feet were quickly lashed to the stirrups. When they started, the skull-headed beast followed them.

'Nice doggie!' Jason said, and for no reason started to laugh. The bearded man turned and scowled at him until he was quiet.

By the time they entered the jungle, it was dark. It was impossible to see under the thick foliage, and they used no lights. The animals seemed to know the way. There were scraping noises and shrill calls from the jungle around them, but it didn't bother Jason too much. Perhaps the automatic manner in which the other man undertook the journey reassured him. Or the presence of the 'dog' that he felt rather than saw. The trip was a long one, but not too uncomfortable.

The regular motion of the animal and his fatigue overcame Jason and he dozed into a fitful sleep, waking with a start each time he slumped forward. In the end, he slept sitting up in the saddle. Hours passed this way, until he opened his eyes and saw a square of light before him. The trip was over.

His legs were stiff and galled with saddle sores. After his feet were untied, getting down was an effort and he almost fell. A door opened and Jason went in. It took his eyes some moments to get used to the light, until he could make out the man on the bed before him.

'Come over here and sit down.' The voice was full and strong, accustomed to command. The body was that of an invalid. A blanket covered him to the waist, above that the flesh was sickly white, spotted with red nodules, and hung loosely over the bones. There seemed to be nothing left of the man except skin and skeleton.

'Not very nice,' the man on the bed said, 'but I've grown used to it.' His tone changed abruptly. 'Naxa said you were from off-world. Is that true?'

Jason nodded yes, and his answer stirred the living skeleton to life. The head lifted from the pillow and the red-rimmed eyes sought his with a desperate intensity.

'My name is Rhes and I'm a . . . grubber. Will you help me?'

Jason wondered at the intensity of Rhes's question, all out of proportion to the simple content of its meaning. Yet he could see no reason to give anything other than the first and obvious answer that sprang to his lips.

'Of course I'll help you, in whatever way I can. As long as it involves no injury to anyone else. What do you want?'

The sick man's head had fallen back limply, exhausted, as Jason talked. But the fire still burned in the eyes.

'Feel assured -- I want to injure no others,' Rhes said. 'Quite the opposite. As you see, I am suffering from a disease that our remedies will not stop. Within a few more days I will be dead. Now I have seen . . . the city people . . . using a device, they press it over a wound or an animal bite. Do you have one of these machines?'

'That sounds like a description of the medikit,' Jason touched the button at his waist that dropped the medikit into his hand. 'I have mine here. It analyses and treats most . . .'

'Would you use it on me?' Rhes broke in, his voice suddenly urgent.

'I'm sorry,' Jason said. 'I should have realized.' He stepped forward and pressed the machine over one of the inflamed areas on Rhes's chest. The operation light came on and the thin shaft of the analyser probe slid down. When it withdrew, the device hummed, then clicked three times as three separate hypodermic needles lanced into the skin. Then the light went out.

'Is that all?' Rhes asked, as he watched Jason stow the medikit back in his belt.

Jason nodded, then looked up and noticed the wet marks of tears on the sick man's face. Rhes became aware of them at the same time and brushed at them angrily.

'When a man is sick,' he growled, 'the body and all its senses become traitor. I don't think I have cried since I was a child – but you must realize it's not myself I'm crying for. It's the untold thousands of my people who have died for lack of that little device you treat so casually.'

'Surely you have medicines, doctors of your own?'

'Herb doctors and witch doctors,' Rhes said, consigning them all to oblivion with a chop of his hand. 'The few hardworking and honest men are hampered by the fact that the faith healers can usually cure better than their strongest potion.'

The talking had tired Rhes. He stopped suddenly and closed his eyes. On his chest, the inflamed areas were already losing their angry colour as the injections took effect. Jason glanced around the room, looking for clues to the mystery of these people.

Floor and walls were made of wood lengths fitted together, free of paint or decoration. They looked simple and crude, fit only for the savages he had expected to meet. Or were they crude? The wood had a sweeping, flame-like grain. When he bent close he saw that wax had been rubbed over the wood to bring out this pattern. Was this the act of savages – or of artistic men seeking to make the most of simple materials? The final effect was far superior to the drab-paint and riveted-steelrooms of the city dwelling Pyrrans. Wasn't it true that both ends of the artistic scale were dominated by simplicity? The untutored Aborigine made a simple expression of a clear idea, and created beauty. At the other extreme, the sophisticated critic rejected over-elaboration and decoration and sought the truthful clarity of uncluttered art. At which end of the scale was he looking now?

These men were savages, he had been told that. They dressed in furs and spoke a slurred and broken language, at least Naxa did. Rhes admitted he preferred faith healers to doctors. But, if all this were true, where did the communicator fit into the picture? Or the glowing ceiling that illuminated the room with a soft light?

Rhes opened his eyes and stared at Jason, as if seeing him for the first time. 'Who are you?' he asked. 'And what are you doing here?'

There was a cold menace in his words, and Jason understood why. The city Pyrrans hated the 'grubbers' and, without a doubt, the feeling was mutual. Naxa's axe had proved that. Naxa had entered silently while they talked, and stood with his fingers touching the haft of this same axe. Jason knew his life was still in jeopardy, until he gave an answer that satisfied these men.

He couldn't tell the truth. If they once suspected he was spying among them to aid the city people, it would be the end. Nevertheless, he had to be free to talk about the survival problem.

The answer hit him as soon as he had stated the problem. All this had only taken an instant to consider, as he turned back to face the invalid, and he answered at once. Trying to keep his voice normal and unconcerned.

'I'm Jason dinAlt, an ecologist, so you see I have the best reasons in the universe for visiting this planet –'

'What is an ecologist?' Rhes broke in. There was nothing in his voice to indicate whether he meant the question seriously, or as a trap. All traces of the ease of their earlier conversation were gone; his voice had the deadliness of a stingwing's poison. Jason chose his words carefully.

'Simply stated, it is that branch of biology that considers the

92

relations between organisms and their environment. How climatic and other factors affect the life forms, and how the life forms in turn affect each other and the environment.' That much Jason knew was true – but he really knew very little more about the subject, so he moved on quickly.

'I heard reports of this planet, and finally came here to study it firsthand. I did what work I could in the shelter of the city, but it wasn't enough. The people there think I'm crazy, but they finally agreed to let me make a trip out here.'

'What arrangements have been made for your return?' Naxa snapped.

'None,' Jason told him. 'They seemed quite sure that I would be killed instantly and had no hope of me coming back. They refused to let me go on my own and I had to break away.'

This answer seemed to satisfy Rhes and his face cracked into a mirthless smile. 'They would think that, those junkmen. Can't move a metre outside their walls without an armour-plated machine big as a barn. What did they tell you about us?'

Again Jason knew a lot depended on his answer. This time he thought carefully before speaking.

'Well, perhaps I'll get that axe in the back of my neck for saying this – but I have to be honest. You must know what they think. They told me you were filthy and ignorant savages – who smelt. And you – well, had curious customs you practised with the animals. In exchange for food, they traded you beads and knives. . . .'

Both Pyrrans broke into a convulsion of laughter at this. Rhes stopped soon, from weakness, but Naxa laughed himself into a coughing fit and had to splash water over his head from a gourd jug.

'That I believe well enough,' Rhes said. 'It sounds like the stupidity they would talk. Those people know nothing of the world they live in. I hope the rest of what you said is true, but even if it is not, you are welcome here. You are from off-world, that I know. No junkman would have lifted a finger to save my life. You are the first off-worlder my people have ever known and for that you are doubly welcome. We will help you in any way we can. My arm is your arm.'

These last words had a ritual sound to them and, when Jason

repeated them, Naxa nodded at the correctness of this. At the same time, Jason felt that they were more than empty ritual. Interdependence meant survival on Pyrrus, and he knew that these people stood together to the death against the mortal dangers around them. He hoped the ritual would include him in that protective sphere.

'That is enough for tonight,' Rhes said. 'The spotted sickness has weakened me, and your medicine has turned me to jelly. You will stay here, Jason. There is a blanket, but no bed, at least for now.'

Enthusiasm had carried Jason this far, making him forget the two-G exertions of the long day. Now fatigue hit him a physical blow. He had dim memories of refusing food and rolling in the blanket on the floor. After that, oblivion.

CHAPTER–SEVENTEEN

Every square inch of his body ached where the doubled gravity had pressed his flesh to the unyielding wood of the floor. His eyes were gummy and his mouth was filled with an indescribable taste that came off in chunks. Sitting up was an effort and he had to stifle a groan as his joints cracked.

'Good day, Jason,' Rhes called from the bed. 'If I didn't believe in medicine so strongly, I would be tempted to say there is a miracle in your machine that has cured me overnight.'

There was no doubt that he was on the mend. The inflamed patches had vanished and the burning light was gone from his eyes. He sat, propped up on the bed, watching the morning sun melt the night's hailstorm into the fields.

'There's meat in the cabinet there,' he said, 'and either water or visk to drink.'

The visk proved to be a distilled beverage of extraordinary potency that instantly cleared the fog from Jason's brain, though it did leave a slight ringing in his ears. And the meat was a tenderly smoked joint, the best food he had tasted since leaving Darkhan. Taken together, they restored his faith in life and the future. He lowered his glass with a relaxed sigh and looked around.

With the pressures of immediate survival and exhaustion removed, his thoughts returned automatically to his problem. What were these people really like–and how had they managed to survive in the deadly wilderness? In the city he had been told they were savages. Yet there was a carefully tended and repaired communicator on the wall. And by the door a crossbow that fired machined metal bolts; he could see the tool marks still visible on their shanks. The one thing he needed was more information. He could start by getting rid of some of his mis-information.

'Rhes, you laughed when I told you what the city people said, about trading you trinkets for food. What do they really trade you?'

'Anything within certain limits,' Rhes said. 'Small manufactured items, such as electronic components for our communicators. Rustless alloys we can't make in our forges, cutting tools, atomic-electric converters that produce power from any radioactive element. Things like that. Within reason they'll trade anything we ask that isn't on the forbidden list. They need the food badly.'

'And the items on the forbidden list –'

'Weapons of course, or anything that might be made into a powerful weapon. They know we make gunpowder so we can't get anything like large casting or seamless tubing we could make into heavy gun barrels. We drill our own rifle barrels by hand, though the crossbow is quieter and faster in the jungle. Then they don't like us to know very much, so the only reading matter that gets to us are tech maintenance manuals, empty of basic theory.

'The last banned category you know about – medicine. This is the one thing I can't understand, that makes me burn with hatred with every death they might have prevented.'

'I know their reasons,' Jason said.

'Then tell me, because I can think of none.'

'Survival – it's just that simple. I doubt if you realize it, but they have a decreasing population. It is just a matter of years before they will be gone. Whereas your people at least must have a stable – if not slightly growing – population to have existed without their mechanical protections. So in the city they hate you and are jealous of you at the same time. If they gave you medicine and you prospered, you would be winning the battle they have lost. I imagine they tolerate you as a necessary evil, to supply them with food, otherwise they wish you were all dead.'

'It makes sense,' Rhes growled, slamming his fist against the bed. 'The kind of twisted logic you expect from junkmen. They use us to feed them, give us the absolute minimum in return, and at the same time cut us off from the knowledge that will get us out of this hand-to-mouth existence. Worse, far worse, they cut us off from the stars and the rest of mankind.' The hatred on his face was so strong that Jason unconsciously drew back.

'Do you think we are savages here, Jason? We act and look like animals because we have to fight for existence on an animal level. Yet we know about the stars. In that chest over there, sealed in metal, are over thirty books, all we have. Fiction most of them, with some history and general science thrown in. Enough to keep alive the stories of the settlement here and the rest of the universe outside. We see the ships land in the city and we know that up there are worlds we can only dream about and never see. Do you wonder that we hate these beasts that call themselves men, and would destroy them in an instant if we could? They are right to keep weapons from us – for sure as the sun rises in the morning we would kill them to a man if we were able, and take over the things they have withheld from us.'

It was a harsh condemnation, but essentially a truthful one. At least from the point of view of the outsiders. Jason didn't try to explain to the angry man that the city Pyrrans looked on their attitude as being the only possible and logical one. 'How did this battle between your two groups ever come about?' he asked.

'I don't know,' Rhes said. 'I've thought about it many times, but there are no records of that period. We do know that we are all descended from colonists who arrived at the same time. Somewhere, at some time, the two groups separated. Perhaps it was a war, I've read about them in the books. I have a partial theory, though I can't prove it, that it was the location of the city.'

'Location – I don't understand.'

'Well, you know the junkmen, and you've seen where their city is. They managed to put it right in the middle of the most savage spot on this planet. You know they don't care about any living thing except themselves; shoot and kill is their only logic. So they wouldn't consider where to build their city, and managed to build it in the stupidest spot imaginable. I'm sure my ancestors saw how foolish this was and tried to tell them so. That would be reason enough for a war, wouldn't it?'

'It might have been – if that's really what happened,' Jason said. 'But I think you have the problem turned backwards. It's a war between native Pyrran life and humans, each fighting to destroy the other. The life forms change continually, seeking that final destruction of the invader.'

'Your theory is even wilder than mine,' Rhes said. 'That's not true at all. I admit that life isn't too easy on this planet – if what I have read in the books about other planets is true – but it doesn't change. You have to be fast on your feet and keep your eyes open for anything bigger than you, but you can survive. Anyway, it doesn't really matter why. The junkmen always look for trouble and I'm happy to see that they have enough.'

Jason didn't try to press the point. The effort of forcing Rhes to change his basic attitudes wasn't worth it – even if possible. He hadn't succeeded in convincing anyone in the city of the lethal mutations even when they could observe all the facts. Rhes could still supply information though.

'I suppose it's not important who started the battle,' Jason said for the other man's benefit, not meaning a word of it. 'But you'll have to agree that the city people are permanently at war with all the local life. Your people, though, have managed to befriend at least two species that I have seen. Do you have any idea how this was done?'

'Naxa will be here in a minute,' Rhes said, pointing to the door, 'as soon as he's taken care of the animals. Ask him. He's the best talker we have.'

'Talker?' Jason asked. 'I had the opposite idea about him. He didn't talk much, and what he did say was, well – a little hard to understand at times.'

'Not that kind of talking,' Rhes broke in impatiently. 'The talkers look after the animals. They train the dogs and doryms, and the better ones like Naxa are always trying to work with other beasts. They dress crudely, but they have to. I've heard them say that the animals don't like chemicals, metal or tanned leather, so they wear untanned furs for the most part. But don't let the dirt fool you, it has nothing to do with his intelligence.'

'Doryms? Are those your carrying beasts – the kind we rode coming here?'

Rhes nodded. 'Doryms are more than pack animals, they're really a little bit of everything. The large males pull the ploughs and other machines, while the younger animals are used for meat. If you want to know more, ask Naxa, you'll find him in the barn.'

'I'd like to do that,' Jason said, standing up. 'Only I feel undressed without my gun–'

'Take it, by all means, it's in that chest by the door. Only watch out what you shoot around here.'

Naxa was in the rear of the barn, filing down one of the spade-like toenails of a dorym. It was a strange scene. The fur-dressed man with a great beast – and the contrast of a beryllium-copper file and electro-luminescent plates lighting the work. The dorym opened its nostrils and pulled away when Jason entered. Naxa patted its neck and talked softly until it quieted and stood still, shivering slightly.

Something stirred in Jason's mind, with the feeling of a long unused muscle being stressed. A hauntingly familiar sensation.

'Good morning,' Jason said. Naxa grunted something and went back to his filing. Watching him for a few minutes, Jason tried to analyse this new feeling. It itched and slipped aside when he reached for it, escaping him. Whatever it was, it had started when Naxa had talked to the dorym.

'Could you call one of the dogs in here, Naxa? I'd like to see one closer up.'

Without raising his head from his work, Naxa gave a low whistle. Jason was sure it couldn't have been heard outside of the barn. Yet within a minute one of the Pyrran dogs slipped quietly in. The talker rubbed the beast's head, mumbling to it, while the animal looked intently into his eyes.

The dog became restless when Naxa turned back to work on the dorym. It prowled around the barn, sniffing, then moved quickly towards the open door. Jason called it back.

At least he meant to call it. At the last moment he said nothing. Nothing aloud. On sudden impulse he kept his mouth closed – only he called the dog with his mind. Thinking the words *Come here*, directing the impulse at the animal with all the force and direction he had ever used to manipulate dice. As he did it, he realized it had been a long time since he had even considered using his *psi* powers.

The dog stopped and turned back towards him.

It hesitated, looking at Naxa, then walked over to Jason.

Seen this closely, the beast was a nightmare hound. The hairless protective plates, tiny red-rimmed eyes, and countless, saliva-dripping teeth did little to inspire confidence. Yet Jason felt no fear. There was a rapport between man and animal that was understood. Without conscious thought, he reached out and scratched the dog along the back, where he knew it itched.

'Di'n't know y're a talker,' Naxa said. As he watched them, there was friendship in his voice for the first time.

'I didn't know either – until just now,' Jason said. He looked into the eyes of the animal before him, scratched the ridged and ugly back, and began to understand.

The talkers must have well-developed *psi* facilities, that was obvious now. There is no barrier of race or alien form when two creatures share each other's emotions. Empathy first, so there would be no hatred or fear. After that direct communication. The talkers might have been the ones who first broke through the barrier of hatred on Pyrrus and learned to live with the native life. Others could have followed their example – this might explain how the community of 'grubbers' had been formed.

Now that he was concentrating on it, Jason was aware of the soft flow of thoughts around him. The consciousness of the dorym was matched by other like patterns from the rear of the

99

barn. He knew without going outside that more of the big beasts were in the field back there.

'This is all new to me,' Jason said. 'Have you ever thought about it, Naxa? What does it feel like to be a talker? I mean, do you *know* why it is you can get the animals to obey you while other people have no luck at all?'

Thinking of this sort troubled Naxa. He ran his fingers through his thick hair and scowled as he answered. 'Nev'r thought about it. Just do it. Just get t'know the beast real good, then y'can guess what they're going t'do. That's all.'

It was obvious that Naxa had never thought about the origin of his ability to control the animals. And if he hadn't, probably no one else had. They had no reason to. They simply accepted the powers of talkers as one of the facts of life.

Ideas slipped towards each other in his mind, like the pieces of a puzzle joining together. He had told Kerk that the native life of Pyrrus had joined in battle against mankind, he didn't know why. Well, he still didn't know why, but he was getting an idea of the 'how'.

'About how far are we from the city?' Jason asked. 'Do you have an idea how long it would take us to get there by dorym?'

'Half a day there – half back. Why? Y'want to go?'

'I don't want to get into the city, not yet. But I would like to get close to it,' Jason told him.

'See what Rhes says,' was Naxa's answer.

Rhes granted instant permission, without asking any questions. They saddled up and left at once, in order to complete the round trip before dark.

They had been travelling less than an hour before Jason knew they were going in the direction of the city. With each minute, the feeling grew stronger. Naxa was aware of it, too, stirring in the saddle with unvoiced feelings. They had to keep touching and reassuring their mounts which were growing skittish and restless.

'This is far enough,' Jason said. Naxa gratefully pulled to a stop.

The wordless thought beat through Jason's mind, filling it. He could feel it on all sides – only much stronger ahead of them in the direction of the unseen city. Naxa and the doryms reacted in the same way, restlessly uncomfortable, not knowing the cause.

One thing was obvious now. The Pyrran animals were sensitive to *psi* radiation – probably the plants and lower life forms as well. Perhaps they communicated by it, since they obeyed the men who had a strong control of it. And in this area was a wash of *psi* radiation such as he had never experienced before. Though his personal talents specialized in psychokinesis – the mental control of inanimate matter – he was still sensitive to most mental phenomena. Watching a sports event, he had many times felt the unanimous accord of many minds expressing the same thought. What he felt now was like that.

Only terribly different. A crowd exulted at some success on the field, or groaned at a failure. The feeling fluxed and changed as the game progressed. Here the wash of thought was unending, strong and frightening. It didn't translate into words very well. It was part hatred, part fear – and all destruction.

'KILL THE ENEMY' was as close as Jason could express it. But it was more than that. An unending river of mental outrage and death.

'Let's go back now,' he said, suddenly battered and sickened by the feelings he had let wash through him. As they started the return trip, he began to understand many things.

His sudden unspeakable fear when the Pyrran animal had attacked him that first day on the planet. And his recurrent nightmares that had never completely ceased, even with drugs. Both of these were his reaction to the hatred directed at the city. Though for some reason he hadn't felt it directly up until now, enough had reached through to him to get a strong emotional reaction.

Rhes was asleep when they got back and Jason couldn't talk to him until morning. In spite of his fatigue from the trip, he stayed awake late into the night, going over in his mind the discoveries of the day. Could he tell Rhes what he had found out? Not very well. If he did that, he would have to explain the importance of his discovery and what he meant to use it for. Nothing that aided the city dwellers would appeal to Rhes in the slightest. Best to say nothing until the entire affair was over.

CHAPTER EIGHTEEN

After breakfast, he told Rhes he wanted to return to the city.

'Then you have seen enough of our barbarian world, and wish to go back to your friends. To help them wipe us out, perhaps?' Rhes said it lightly, but there was a touch of cold malice behind his words.

'I hope you don't really think that,' Jason told him. 'You must realize that the opposite is true. I would like to see this civil war ended and your people getting all the benefits of science and medicine that have been withheld. I'll do everything I can to bring that about.'

'They'll never change,' Rhes said gloomily, 'so don't waste your time. But there is one thing you must do, for your protection and ours. Don't admit, or even hint, that you've talked to any grubbers!'

'Why not!'

'Why not –! Suffering death, are you that simple! They will do anything to see that we don't rise too high, and would much prefer to see us all dead. Do you think they would hesitate to kill you if they as much as suspected you had contacted us? They realize – even if you don't – that you can single-handedly alter the entire pattern of power on this planet. The ordinary junkman may think of us as being only one step above the animals, but the leaders don't. They know what we need and what we want. They could probably guess just what it is I am going to ask you.

'Help us, Jason dinAlt. Get back among those human pigs and lie. Say you never talked to us, that you hid in the forest and we attacked you and you had to shoot to save yourself. We'll supply some recent corpses to make that part of your story sound good. Make them believe you and, even after you think you have them convinced, keep on acting the part because they will be watching you. Then tell them you have finished your work and are ready to leave. Get safely off Pyrus, to another planet, and I promise you anything in the universe. Whatever you want you shall have. Power, money — *anything*.

'This is a rich planet. The junkmen mine and sell the metal, but we could do it much better. Bring a spaceship back here and land anywhere on this continent. We have no cities, but our people have farms everywhere, they will find you. We will then have commerce, trade — on our own. This is what we all want and we will work hard for it. And *you* will have done it. Whatever you want, we will give. That is a promise and we do not break our promises.'

The intensity and magnitude of what he described rocked Jason. He knew that Rhes spoke the truth and the entire resources of the planet would be his; if he did as asked. For one second he was tempted, savouring the thought of what it would be like. Then came realization that it would be a half power, and a poor one at that. If these people had the strength they wanted, their first act would be the attempted destruction of the city men. The result would be bloody civil war that would probably destroy them both. Rhes's answer was a good one — but only half an answer.

Jason had to find a better solution. One that would stop *all* the fighting on this planet and allow the two groups of humans to live in peace.

'I will do nothing to injure your people, Rhes — and everything in my power to aid them,' Jason said.

This half answer satisfied Rhes, who could see only one interpretation of it. He spent the rest of the morning on the communicator, arranging for the food supplies that were being brought to the trading site.

'The supplies are ready and we have sent the signal,' he said. 'The truck will be here tomorrow and you will be waiting for it. Everything is arranged as I told you. You'll leave now with Naxa. You must reach the meeting-spot before the trucks.'

CHAPTER NINETEEN

'Trucks almost here. Y'know what to do?' Naxa asked.

Jason nodded, and looked again at the dead man. Some beast had torn his arm off and he had bled to death. The severed arm had been tied into the shirt sleeve, so from a distance it looked normal. Seen close up, this limp arm, plus the white skin and shocked expression on the face, gave Jason an unhappy sensation. He liked to see his corpses safely buried. However, he could understand its importance today.

'Here they're. Wait until his back's turned,' Naxa whispered.

The armoured truck had three powered trailers in tow this time. The train ground up the rock slope and whined to a stop. Krannon climbed out of the cab and looked carefully around before opening up the trailers. He had a lift robot along to help him with the loading.

'*Now!*' Naxa hissed.

Jason burst into the clearing, running, shouting Krannon's name. There was a crackling behind him as two of the hidden men hurled the corpse through the foliage after him. He turned and fired without stopping, setting the thing afire in mid-air.

There was a crack of another gun as Krannon fired; his shot jarred the twice-dead corpse before it hit the ground. Then he was lying prone, firing into the trees behind the running Jason.

Just as Jason reached the truck, there was a whirring in the air and hot pain ripped into his back, throwing him to the ground. He looked around as Krannon dragged him through the door, and saw the metal shaft of a cross-bow bolt sticking out of his shoulder.

'Lucky,' the Pyrran said. 'An inch lower would have got your heart. I warned you about those grubbers. You're lucky to get off with only this.' He lay next to the door and snapped shots into the now quiet wood.

Taking out the bolt hurt much more than it had going in. Jason cursed the pain as Krannon put on a dressing, and admired the singleness of purpose of the people who had shot him. They had risked his life to make his escape look real. And also risked the chance that he might turn against them after being shot. They did a job completely and thoroughly and he cursed them for their efficiency.

Krannon climbed warily out of the truck, after Jason was bandaged. Finishing the loading quickly, he started the train of trailers back towards the city. Jason had an anti-pain shot and dozed off as soon as they started.

While he slept, Krannon must have radioed ahead, because Kerk was waiting when they arrived. As soon as the truck entered the perimeter, he threw open the door and dragged Jason out. The bandage pulled and Jason felt the wound tear open. He ground his teeth together; Kerk would not have the satisfaction of hearing him cry out.

'I told you to stay in the buildings until the ship left. Why did you leave? Why did you go outside? You talked to the grubbers – didn't you?' With each question he shook Jason again.

'I didn't talk to – anyone.' Jason managed to get the words out. 'They tried to take me, I shot two – hid out until the trucks came back.'

'Got another one then,' Krannon said. 'I saw it. Good shooting. Think I got some too. Let him go, Kerk, they shot him in the back before he could reach the truck.'

That's enough explanations, Jason thought to himself. *Don't overdo it. Let him make up his mind later. Now's the time to change the subject. There's one thing that will get his mind off the grubbers.*

'I've been fighting your war for you, Kerk, while you stayed safely inside the perimeter.' Jason leaned back against the side of the truck as the other loosened his grip. 'I've found out what your battle with this planet is really about – and how you can win it. Now let me sit down and I'll tell you.'

More Pyrrans had come up while they talked. None of them moved now. Like Kerk, they stood frozen, looking at Jason. When Kerk talked, he spoke for all of them.

'*What do you mean?*'

'Just what I said. Pyrrus is fighting you – actively and consciously. Get far enough out from this city and you can feel the waves of hatred that are directed at it. No, that's wrong – you can't because you've grown up with it. But I can, and so could anyone else with any sort of *psi* sensitivity. There is a message of war being beamed against you constantly. The life forms of this planet are *psi*-sensitive, and respond to that order. They attack and change and mutate for your destruction. And they'll keep on doing so until you are all dead. Unless you can stop the war.'

'How?' Kerk snapped the word and every face echoed the question.

'By finding whoever or whatever is sending that message. The life forms that attack you have no reasoning intelligence. They are being ordered to do so. I think I know how to find the source of these orders. After that, it will be a matter of getting across a message, asking for a truce and an eventual end to all hostilities.'

A dead silence followed his words as the Pyrrans tried to comprehend the ideas. Kerk moved first, waving them all away.

'Go back to your work. This is my responsibility and I'll take care of it. As soon as I find out what truth there is here – if any – I'll make a complete report.' The people drifted away silently, looking back as they went.

CHAPTER TWENTY

'From the beginning now,' Kerk said. 'And leave out nothing.'

'There is very little more that I can add to the physical facts. I saw the animals, understood the message. I even experimented with some of them and they reacted to my mental commands. What I must do now is track down the source of the orders that keep this war going.

'I'll tell you something that I have never told anyone else. I'm not only lucky at gambling. I have enough *psi* ability to alter probability in my favour. It's an erratic ability that I have tried to improve for obvious reasons. During the past ten years I managed to study at all of the centres that do *psi* research.

106

Compared to other fields of knowledge it is amazing how little they know. Basic *psi* talents can be improved by practice, and some machines have been devised that act as *psi*onic amplifiers. One of these, used correctly, is a very good directional indicator.'

'You want to build this machine?' Kerk asked.

'Exactly. Build it and take it outside the city in the ship. Any signal strong enough to keep this centuries-old battle going should be strong enough to track down. I'll follow it, contact the creatures who are sending it, and try to find out why they are doing it. I assume you'll go along with any reasonable plan that will end this war?'

'Anything reasonable,' Kerk said coldly. 'How long will it take you to build this machine?'

'Just a few days, if you have all the parts here,' Jason told him.

'Then do it. I'm cancelling the flight that's leaving now and I'll keep the ship here, ready to go. When the machine is built, I want you to track the signal and report back to me.'

'Agreed,' Jason said, standing up. 'As soon as I have this hole in my back looked at, I'll draw up a list of things needed.'

A grim, unsmiling man named Skop was assigned to Jason as a combination guide and guard. He took his job very seriously, and it didn't take Jason long to realize that he was a prisoner-at-large. Kerk had accepted his story, but that was no guarantee that he believed it. At a single word from him, the guard could turn executioner.

The chill thought hit Jason that undoubtedly this was what would eventually happen. Whether Kerk accepted the story or not, he couldn't afford to take a chance. As long as there was the slightest possibility Jason had contacted the grubbers, he could not be allowed to leave the planet alive. The woods people were being simple if they thought a plan this obvious might succeed. Or had they just gambled on the very long chance it might work? *They* certainly had nothing to lose by it.

Only half of Jason's mind was occupied with the work as he drew up a list of materials he would need for the *psi*onic direction finder. His thoughts plodded in tight circles, searching for a way out that didn't exist. He was too deeply involved now to just leave. Kerk would see to that. Unless he could find a way to end the war and settle the grubber question, he was marooned on Pyrrus for life. A very short life.

When the list was ready, he called Supply. With a few substitutions, everything he might possibly need was in stock, and would be sent over. Skop sank into an apparent doze in his chair and Jason, his head propped against the pull of gravity by one arm, began a working sketch of his machine.

Jason looked up suddenly, aware of the silence. He could hear machinery in the building and voices in the hall outside. What kind of silence then –?

Mental silence. He had been so preoccupied since his return to the city that he hadn't noticed the complete lack of any kind of *psi* sensation. The constant wash of animal reaction was missing, as was the vague tactile awareness of his PK. With sudden realization, he remembered that it was always this way inside the city.

He tried to listen with his mind – and stopped almost before he began. There was a constant press of thought about him that he was made aware of when he reached out. It was like being in a vessel far beneath the ocean, with your hand on the door that held back the frightening pressure. Touching the door, without opening it, you could feel the stresses, the power pushing in and waiting to crush you. It was this way with the *psi* pressure in the city. The unvoiced hate-filled screams of Pyrrus would instantly destroy any mind that received them. Some function of his brain acted as a *psi* circuit breaker, shutting off awareness before his mind could be blasted. There was just enough leak-through to keep him aware of the pressure – and supply the raw materials for his constant nightmares.

There was only one fringe benefit. The lack of thought pressure made it easier for him to concentrate. In spite of his fatigue, the diagram developed swiftly.

Meta arrived late that afternoon, bringing the parts he had ordered. She slid the long box on to the work bench, started to speak, but changed her mind and said nothing. Jason looked up at her and smiled.

'Confused?' he asked.

'I don't know what you mean,' she said. 'I'm not confused.

Just annoyed. The regular trip has been cancelled and our supply schedule will be thrown off for months to come. And instead of piloting or perimeter assignment all I am allowed to do is stand around and wait for you. Then take some silly flight following your directions. Do you wonder that I'm annoyed?'

Jason carefully set the parts out on the chassis before he spoke. 'As I said, you're confused. I can point out how you're confused – which will make you even more confused. A temptation that I frankly find hard to resist.'

She looked across the bench at him, frowning, one finger unconsciously curling and uncurling a short lock of hair. Jason liked her this way. As a Pyrran operating at full blast, she had as much personality as a gear in a machine. Once out of that pattern she reminded him more of the girl he had known on that first flight to Pyrrus. He wondered if it was possible to really get across to her what he meant.

'I'm not being insulting when I say "confused", Meta. With your background you couldn't be any other way. You have an insular personality. Admittedly, Pyrrus is an unusual island with a lot of high-power problems that you are an expert at solving. That doesn't make it any less of an island. When you face a cosmopolitan problem, you are confused. Or even worse, when your island problems are put into a bigger context. That's like playing your own game, only having the rules change constantly as you go along.'

'You're talking nonsense,' she snapped at him. 'Pyrrus isn't an island and battling for survival is definitely not a game.'

'I'm sorry,' he smiled. 'I was using a figure of speech, and a badly chosen one at that. Let's put the problem on more concrete terms. Take an example. Suppose I were to tell you that over there, hanging from the door-frame, was a stingwing –'

Meta's gun was pointing at the door before he finished the last word. There was a crash as the guard's chair went over. He had jumped from a half-doze to full alertness in an instant, his gun also searching the door-frame.

'That was just an example,' Jason said. 'There's really nothing there.' The guard's gun vanished and he scowled a look of contempt at Jason, as he righted the chair and dropped into it.

'You both have proved yourself capable of handling a Pyrran problem,' Jason continued. 'But what if I said that there is a thing hanging from the door-frame that *looks* like a stingwing, but is really a kind of large insect that spins a fine silk that can be used to weave clothes?'

The guard glared from under his thick eyebrows at the empty door-frame, his gun whined part way out, then snapped back into the holster. He growled something inaudible at Jason, then stamped into the outer room, slamming the door behind him. Meta frowned in concentration and looked puzzled.

'It couldn't be anything except a stingwing,' she finally said. 'Nothing else could possibly look like that. And even if it did spin silk, it would bite if you got near, so you would have to kill it.' She smiled with satisfaction at the indestructible logic of her answer.

'Wrong again,' Jason said. 'I just described the mimic-spinner that lives on Stover's Planet. It imitates the most violent forms of life there, does such a good job that it has no need for other defences. It'll sit quietly on your hand and spin for you by the yard. If I dropped a shipload of them here on Pyrrus you never could be sure when to shoot, could you?'

'But they are not here now,' Meta insisted.

'Yet they could be quite easily. And if they were, all the rules of your game would change. Getting the idea now? There are some fixed laws and rules in the galaxy – but they're not the ones you live by. Your rule is war unending with the local life. I want to step outside your rule book and end that war. Wouldn't you like that? Wouldn't you like an existence that was more than just an endless battle for survival? A life with a chance for happiness, love, music, art – all the enjoyable things you have never had the time for.'

All the Pyrran sternness was gone from her face as she listened to what he said, letting herself follow these alien concepts. He had put his hand out automatically as he talked, and had taken hers. It was warm and her pulse fast to his touch.

Meta suddenly became conscious of his hand and snapped hers away, rising to her feet at the same time. As she started blindly towards the door, Jason's voice snapped after her.

'The guard, Skop, ran away because he didn't want to lose

his precious two-value logic. It's all he has. But you've seen other parts of the galaxy, Meta, you know there is a lot more to life than kill-and-be-killed on Pyrrus. You feel it is true, even if you won't admit it.'

She turned and ran out of the door.

Jason looked after her, his hand scraping the bristle on his chin thoughtfully. 'Meta, I have the faint hope that the woman is winning over the Pyrran. I think that I saw – perhaps for the first time in the history of this bloody, war-torn city – a tear in one of it's citizen's eyes.'

CHAPTER TWENTY-ONE

'Drop that equipment and Kerk will undoubtedly pull both your arms off,' Jason said. 'He's over there now, looking as sorry as possible that I ever talked him into this.'

Skop cursed under the bulky mass of the *psi* detector, passing it up to Meta who waited in the open port of the spaceship. Jason supervised the loading and blasted all the local life that came to investigate. Horndevils were thick this morning and he shot four of them. He was last aboard and closed the lock behind him.

'Where are you going to install it?' Meta asked.

'You tell me,' Jason said. 'I need a spot for the antenna where there will be no dense metal in front of the bowl to interfere with the signal. Thin plastic will do or, if worst comes to worst, I can mount it outside the hull with a remote drive.'

'You may have to,' she said. 'The hull is an unbroken unit; we do all viewing by screen and instruments. I don't think – wait – there is one place that might do.'

She led the way to a bulge in the hull that marked one of the lifeboats. They went in through the always-open lock, Skop struggling after them with the apparatus.

'These lifeboats are half-buried in the ship,' Meta explained. 'They have transparent front ports covered by friction shields that withdraw automatically when the boat is launched.'

'Can we pull back the shields now?'

'I think so,' she said. She traced the launching circuits to a junction box and opened the lid. When she closed the shield relay manually, the heavy plates slipped back into the hull. There was a clear view, since most of the viewport projected beyond the parent ship.

'Perfect,' Jason said. 'I'll set up here. Now how do I talk to you in the ship?'

'Right here,' she said. 'There's a pre-tuned setting on this communicator. Don't touch anything else – and particularly not this switch.' She pointed to a large pull-handle set square into the centre of the control board. 'Emergency launching. Two seconds after that is pulled, the lifeboat is shot free. And it so happens this boat has no fuel.'

'Hands off for sure,' Jason said. 'Now have Husky there run me in a line with ship's power and I'll get this stuff set up.'

The detector was simple, though the tuning had to be precise. A dish-shaped antenna pulled in the signal for the delicately balanced detector. There was a sharp fall-off on both sides of the input so direction could be precisely determined. The resulting signal was fed to an amplifier stage. Unlike the electronic components of the first stage, this one was drawn in symbols on white paper. Carefully glued-on input and output leads ran to it.

When everything was ready and clamped into place, Jason nodded to Meta's image on the screen. 'Take her up – and easy, please. None of your nine-G specials. Go into a slow circle around the perimeter, until I tell you differently.'

Under steady power the ship lifted and grabbed for altitude, then eased into its circular course. They made five circuits of the city before Jason shook his head.

'The thing seems to be working fine, but we're getting too much noise from all the local life. Get thirty kilometres out from the city and start a new circuit.'

The results were better this time. A powerful signal came, from the direction of the city, confined to less than a degree of arc. With the antenna fixed at a right angle to the direction of the ship's flight, the signal was fairly constant. Meta rotated the ship on its main axis, until Jason's lifeboat was directly below.

'Going fine now,' he said. 'Just hold your controls as they are and keep the nose from drifting.'

After making a careful mark on the setting circle, Jason turned the receiving antenna through 180° of arc. As the ship kept to its circle, he made a slow collecting sweep of any signals beamed at the city. They were half-way around before he got a new signal.

It was there all right, narrow but strong. Just to be sure, he let the ship complete two more sweeps, and he noted the direction on the gyrocompass each time. They coincided. The third time around he called to Meta.

'Get ready for a full right turn, or whatever you call it. I think I have our bearing. Get ready – *now*.'

It was a slow turn and Jason never lost the signal. A few times it wavered, but he brought it back on. When the compass settled down, Meta pushed on more power.

They set their course towards the native Pyrrans.

An hour's flight at close to top atmospheric speed brought no change. Meta complained, but Jason kept her on course. The signal never varied and was slowly picking up strength. They crossed the chain of volcanoes that marked the continental limits, the ship bucking in the fierce thermals. Once the shore was behind and they were over water, Skop joined Meta in grumbling. He kept his turret spinning, but there was very little to shoot at this far from land.

When the islands came over the horizon, the signal began to dip.

'Slow now,' Jason called. 'Those islands ahead look like our source!'

A continent had been here once, floating on Pyrrus's liquid core. Pressures changed, land masses shifted, and the continent had sunk beneath the ocean. All that was left now of the teeming life of that land mass was confined to a chain of islands, once the mountain peaks of the highest range of mountains. These islands, whose sheer sides rose straight from the water, held the last inhabitants of the lost continent. The weeded-out descendants of the victors of uncountable violent contests. Here lived the oldest native Pyrrans.

'Come in lower,' Jason signalled, 'towards that large peak. The signals seem to originate there.'

They swooped low over the mountain, but nothing was visible other than the trees and sunblasted rock.

The pain almost took Jason's head off. A blast of hatred that drove through the amplifier and into his skull. He tore off the phones and clutched his skull between his hands. Through watering eyes, he saw the black cloud of flying beasts hurtle up from the trees below. He had a single glimpse of the hillside beyond before Meta blasted power to the engines and the ship leaped away.

'We've found them!' Her fierce exultation faded as she saw Jason through the communicator. 'Are you all right? What happened?'

'Feel . . . burned out. . . . I've felt a *psi* blast before, but nothing like that! I had a glimpse of an opening, looked like a cave mouth, just before the blast hit. Seemed to come from there.'

'Lie down,' Meta said. 'I'll get you back as fast as I can. I'm calling ahead to Kerk. He has to know what happened.'

A group of men were waiting in the landing-station when they came down. They stormed out as soon as the ship touched, shielding their faces from the still-hot tubes. Kerk burst in as soon as the port was cracked, peering around until he spotted Jason stretched out on an acceleration couch.

'Is it true?' he barked. 'You've traced the alien criminals who started this war?'

'Slow, man, slow,' Jason said. 'I've traced the source of the *psi* message that keeps your war going. I've found no evidence as to who started this war, and certainly wouldn't go so far as to call them criminals. . . .'

'I'm tired of your word-play,' Kerk broke in. 'You've found these creatures and their location has been marked.'

'On the chart,' Meta said, 'I could fly there blindfolded.'

'Fine, fine,' Kerk said, rubbing his hands together so hard they could hear the harsh rasp of the callouses. 'It takes a real effort to grasp the idea that, after all these centuries, the war might be coming to an end. But it's possible now. Instead of simply killing off these self-renewing legions of the damned that attack us, we can get to the leaders. Search them out, carry the war to them for a change – and blast their strain from the face of this planet!'

'Nothing of the sort!' Jason said, sitting up with an effort. 'Nothing doing! Since I came to this planet I have been knocked around, and risked my life ten times over. Do you think I have done this just to satisfy your bloodthirsty ambitions? It's peace I'm after – not destruction. You promised to contact these creatures, attempt to negotiate with them. Aren't you a man of honour who keeps his word?'

'I'll ignore the insult – though I'd have killed you for it at any other time,' Kerk said. 'You've been of great service to our people, we are not ashamed to acknowledge an honest debt. At the same time, do not accuse me of breaking promises that I never made. I recall my exact words. I promised to go along with any reasonable plan that would end this war. That is just what I intend to do. Your plan to negotiate a peace is not reasonable. Therefore we are going to destroy the enemy.'

'Think first,' Jason called after Kerk, who had turned to leave. 'What is wrong with trying negotiation or an armistice? Then, if that fails, you can try your way.'

The compartment was getting crowded as other Pyrrans pushed in. Kerk, almost to the door, turned to face Jason.

'I'll tell you what's wrong with armistice,' he said. 'It's a coward's way out, that's what it is. It's all right for you to suggest it, you're from off-world and don't know any better. But do you honestly think I could entertain such a defeatist notion for one instant? When I speak, I speak not only for myself, but for all of us here. We don't mind fighting, and we know how to do it. We know that if this war was over, we could build a better world here. At the same time, if we have the choice of continued war or a cowardly peace – *we vote for war*. This war will only be over when the enemy is utterly destroyed!'

The listening Pyrrans murmured in agreement, and Jason had to shout to be heard above them. 'That's really wonderful. I bet you even think it's original. But don't you hear all that cheering offstage? Those are the spirits of every sabre-rattling son-of-a-bitch that ever plugged for noble war. They even

115

recognize the old slogan. We're on the side of light, and the enemy is a creature of darkness. And it doesn't matter a damn if the other side is saying the same thing. You've still got the same old words that have been killing people since the birth of the human race. A "cowardly peace", that's a good one. Peace means not being at war, not fighting. How can you have a cowardly not-fighting. What are you trying to hide with this semantic confusion? Your real reasons? I can't blame you for being ashamed of them – I would be. Why don't you just come out and say you are keeping the war going because you enjoy killing? Seeing things die makes you and your murderers happy, and you want to make them happier still!'

There was a sense but unvoiced pressure in the silence. They waited for Kerk to speak. He was white-faced with anger, held tightly under control.

'You're right, Jason. We like to kill. And we're going to kill. Everything on this planet that ever fought us is going to die. We're going to enjoy doing it very much.'

He turned and left while the weight of his words still hung in the air. The rest followed, talking excitedly. Jason slumped back on the couch, exhausted and defeated.

When he looked up they were gone – all except Meta. She had the same look of bloodthirsty elation as the others, but it drained away when she glanced at him.

'What about it, Meta?' he snapped. 'No doubts? Do you think that destruction is the only way to end this war?'

'I don't know,' she said. 'I can't be sure. For the first time in my life, I find myself with more than one answer to the same question.'

'Congratulations,' he said bitterly. 'It's a sign of growing up.'

CHAPTER TWENTY-TWO

Jason stood to one side and watched the deadly cargo being loaded into the hold of the ship. The Pyrrans were in good humour as they stowed away riot guns, grenades and gas bombs. When the back-pack atom bomb was put aboard, one of them broke into a marching song, and the others picked it up. Maybe they were happy, but the approaching carnage only filled Jason with an intense gloom. He felt that somehow he was a traitor to life. Perhaps the life form he had found needed destroying – and perhaps it didn't. Without making the slightest attempt at conciliation, destruction would be plain murder.

Kerk came out of the operations building and the starter pumps could be heard whining inside the ship. They would leave within minutes. Jason forced himself into a foot-dragging rush and met Kerk half-way to the ship.

'I'm coming with you, Kerk. You owe me at least that much for finding them.'

Kerk hesitated, not liking the idea. 'This is an operational mission,' he said. 'No room for observers, and the extra weight. ... And it's late to stop us, Jason, you know that.'

'You Pyrrans are the worst liars in the universe,' Jason said. 'We both know that ship can lift ten times the amount it's carrying today. Now, do you let me come, or forbid me without reason at all?'

'Get aboard,' Kerk said. 'But keep out of the way or you'll get trampled.'

This time, with a definite destination ahead, the flight was much faster. Meta took the ship into the stratosphere, in a high ballistic arc that ended at the islands. Kerk was in the co-pilot's seat, Jason sat behind them where he could watch the screens. The landing party, twenty-five volunteers, were in the hold below with the weapons. All the screens in the ship were switched to the forward viewer. They watched the green island appear and swell, then vanish behind the flames of the braking rockets. Jockeying the ship carefully, Meta brought it down on a flat shelf near the cave mouth.

Jason was ready this time for the blast of mental hatred – but it still hurt. The gunners laughed and killed gleefully as every animal on the island closed in on the ship. They were slaughtered by the thousands, and still more came.

'Do you have to do this?' Jason asked. 'It's murder, carnage, just butchering those beasts like that.'

'Self-defence,' Kerk said. 'They attack us and they get

killed. What could be simpler. Now shut up or I'll throw you out there with them.'

It was a half an hour before the gunfire slackened. Animals still attacked them, but the mass assaults seemed to be over. Kerk spoke into the intercom.

'Landing party away – and watch your step. They know we're here and will make it as hot as they can. Take the bomb into that cave and see how far back it runs. We can always blast them from the air, but it'll do no good if they're dug into solid rock. Keep your screen open, leave the bomb and pull back at once if I tell you to. Now move.'

The men swarmed down the ladders and formed into open battle-formation. They were soon under attack, but the beasts were picked off before they could get close. It didn't take long for the man at point to reach the cave. He had his pick-up trained in front of him, and the watchers in the ship followed the advance.

'Big cave,' Kerk grunted. 'Slants back and down. What I was afraid of. Bomb dropped on that would just close it up. With no guarantee that anything sealed in it couldn't eventually get out. We'll have to see how far down it goes.'

There was enough heat in the cave now to use the infra-red filters. The rock walls stood out harshly black and white as the advances continued.

'No signs of life since entering the cave,' the officer reported. 'Gnawed bones at the entrance and some bat droppings. It looks like a natural cave – so far.'

Step by step the advance continued, slowing as it went. Insensitive as the Pyrrans were to *psi* pressure, even they were aware of the blast of hatred being continuously levelled at them. Jason, back in the ship, had a headache that slowly grew worse instead of better.

'*Watch out!*' Kerk shouted, staring at the screen with horror.

The cave was filled from wall to wall with pallid, eyeless animals. They poured from tiny side passages and seemed to literally emerge from the ground. Their front ranks dissolved in flame, but more kept pressing in. On the screen the watchers in the ship saw the cave spin dizzily as the operator fell. Pale bodies washed up and concealed the lens.

'Close ranks – flamethrowers and gas!' Kerk bellowed into the mike.

Less than half of the men were alive after that first attack. The survivors, protected by the flamethrowers, set off the gas grenades. Their sealed battle armour protected them while the section of cave filled with gas. Someone dug through the bodies of their attackers and found the pick-up.

'Leave the bomb there and withdraw,' Kerk ordered. 'We've had enough losses already.'

A different man stared out of the screen. The officer was dead. 'Sorry, sir,' he said, 'but it will be just as easy to push ahead as back as long as the gas grenades hold out. We're too close now to pull back.'

'That's an order,' Kerk shouted, but the man was gone from the screen and the advance continued.

Jason's fingers hurt where he had them clamped to the chair arm. He pulled them loose and massaged them. On the screen the black-and-white cave flowed steadily towards them. Minute after minute went by this way. Each time the animals attacked again, a few more gas grenades were used up.

'Something ahead – looks different,' the panting voice cracked from the speaker. The narrow cave slowly opened out into a gigantic chamber, so large that the roof and far walls were lost in the distance.

'What are those?' Kerk asked. 'Get a searchlight over to the right there.'

The picture on the screen was fuzzy and hard to see now, dimmed by the layers of rock in between. Details couldn't be made out clearly, but it was obvious this was something unusual.

'Never saw – anything quite like them before,' the speaker said. 'Look like big plants of some kind, ten metres tall at least – yet they're moving. Those branches, tentacles or whatever they are, keep pointing towards us and I get the darkest feeling in my head. . . .'

'Blast one, see what happens,' Kerk said.

The gun fired and at the same instant an intensified wave of mental hatred rolled over the men, dropping them to the ground. They rolled in pain, blacked out and unable to think or fight the underground beasts that poured over them in renewed attack.

In the ship, far above, Jason felt the shock to his mind and wondered how the men below could have lived through it. The others in the control room had been hit by it as well. Kerk pounded on the frame of the screen and shouted to the unhearing men below.

'Pull back, come back. . . .'

It was too late. The men only stirred slightly as the victorious Pyrran animals washed over them, clawing for the joints in their armour. Only one man moved, standing up and beating the creatures away with his bare hands. He stumbled a few feet and bent over the writhing mass below him. With a heave of his shoulders, he pulled another man up. The man was dead but his shoulder pack was still strapped to his back. Bloody fingers fumbled at the pack, then both men were washed back under the wave of death.

'That was the bomb!' Kerk shouted to Meta. 'If he didn't change the setting, it's still on ten-second minimum. Get out of here!'

Jason had just time to fall back on the acceleration couch before the rockets blasted. The pressure leaned on him and kept mounting. Vision blacked out but he didn't lose consciousness. Air screamed across the hull, then the sound stopped as they left the atmosphere behind.

Just as Meta cut the power, a glare of white light burst from the screens. They turned black instantly as the hull pick-ups burned out. She switched filters into place, then pressed the button that rotated new pick-ups into position.

Far below, in the boiling sea, a climbing cloud of mushroom-shaped flame filled the spot where the island had been seconds before. The three of them looked at it, silent and unmoving. Kerk recovered first.

'Head for home, Meta, and get operations on the screen. Twenty-five men dead, but they did their job. They knocked out those beasts – whatever they were – and ended the war. I can't think of a better way for a man to die.'

Meta set the orbit, then called operations.

'Trouble getting through,' she said. 'I have a robot landing-beam response, but no one is answering the call.'

A man appeared on the empty screen. He was beaded with sweat and had a harried look in his eyes. 'Kerk,' he said, 'is that you? Get the ship back here at once. We need her fire-power at the perimeter. All blazes broke loose a minute ago, a general attack from every side, worse than I've ever seen.'

'What do you mean?' Kerk stammered in unbelief. 'The war is over. We blasted them, destroyed their headquarters completely.'

'The war is going like it never has gone before,' the other snapped back. 'I don't know what you did, but it stirred up the stewpot of hell here. Now stop talking and get the ship back!'

Kerk turned slowly to face Jason, his face pulled back in a look of raw animal savagery.

'You! You did it! I should have killed you the first time I saw you. I wanted to, now I know I was right. You've been like a plague since you came here, sowing death in every direction. I knew you were wrong, yet I let your twisted words convince me. And look what has happened. First you killed Welf. Then you murdered those men in the cave. Now this attack on the perimeter – all who die there, you will have killed!'

Kerk advanced on Jason, step by slow step, hatred twisting his features. Jason backed away until he could retreat no farther, his shoulders against the chart case. Kerk's hand lashed out, not a fighting blow, but an open slap. Though Jason rolled with it, it still battered him and stretched him full length on the floor. His arm was against the chart case, his fingers near the sealed tubes that held the jump matrices.

Jason seized one of the heavy tubes with both hands and pulled it out. He swung it with all his strength into Kerk's face. It broke the skin on his cheekbone and forehead and blood ran from the cuts. But it didn't slow or stop the big man in the slightest. His smile held no mercy as he reached down and dragged Jason to his feet.

'Fight back,' he said, 'I will have that much more pleasure as I kill you.' He drew back the granite fist that would tear Jason's head from his shoulders.

'Go ahead,' Jason said and stopped struggling. 'Kill me.

You can do it easily. Only don't call it justice. Welf died to save me. But the men on the island died because of your stupidity. I wanted peace and you wanted war. Now you have it. Kill me to soothe your conscience, because the truth is something you can't face up to.'

With a bellow of rage, Kerk drove the pile-driver fist down.

Meta grabbed the arm in both her hands and hung on, pulling it aside before the blow could land. The three of them fell together, half crushing Jason.

'Don't do it,' she screamed. 'Jason didn't want those men to go down there. That was your idea. You can't kill him for that!'

Kerk, exploding with rage, was past hearing. He turned his attention to Meta, tearing her from him. She was a woman and her supple strength was meagre compared to his great muscles. But she was a Pyrran woman and she did what no off-worlder could. She slowed him for a moment, stopped the fury of his attack until he could rip her hands loose and throw her aside. It didn't take him long to do this, but it was just time enough for Jason to get to the door.

Jason stumbled through and jammed shut the lock behind him. A split second after he had driven the bolt home, Kerk's weight plunged into the door. The metal screamed and bent, giving way. One hinge was torn loose and the other held only by a shred of metal. It would go down on the next blow.

Jason wasn't waiting for that. He hadn't stayed to see if the door would stop the raging Pyrran. No door on the ship could stop him. Fast as possible, Jason went down the gangway. There was no safety on the ship, which meant he had to get off it. The lifeboat deck was just ahead.

Ever since first seeing them, he had given a lot of thought to the lifeboats. Though he hadn't looked ahead to this situation, he knew a time might come when he would need transportation of his own. The lifeboats had seemed to be the best bet, except that Meta had told him they had no fuel. She had been right in one thing; the boat he had been in had empty tanks, he had checked. There were five other boats, though, that he hadn't examined. He had wondered about the idea of useless lifeboats and come to what he hoped was a correct conclusion.

This spaceship was the only one the Pyrrans had. Meta had told him once that they always had planned to buy another ship, but never did. Some other necessary war expense managed to come up first. One ship was really enough for their uses. The only difficulty lay in the fact they had to keep that ship in operation or the Pyrran city was dead. Without supplies they would be wiped out in a few months. Therefore the ship's crew couldn't conceive of abandoning their ship. No matter what kind of trouble she got into, they couldn't leave her. When the ship died, so did their world.

With this kind of thinking, there was no need to keep the lifeboats fuelled. Not all of them, at least. Though it stood to reason at least one of them held fuel for short flights that would have been wasteful for the parent ship. At this point, Jason's chain of logic grew weak. Too many 'ifs'. *If* they used the lifeboat at all, one of them should be fuelled. *If* they did, it would be fuelled now. And *if* it were fuelled – which one of the six would it be? Jason had no time to go looking. He had to be right the first time.

His reasoning had supplied him with an answer, the last of a long line of suppositions. If a boat were fuelled, it should be the one nearest the control cabin. The one he was diving towards now. His life depended on this string of guesses.

Behind him the door went down with a crash. Kerk bellowed and leaped. Jason hurled himself through the lifeboat port with the nearest thing to a run he could manage under the doubled gravity. With both hands he grabbed the emergency launching handle and pulled down.

An alarm bell rang and the port slammed shut, literally in Kerk's face. Only his Pyrran reflexes saved him from being smashed by it.

Solid fuel launchers exploded and blasted the lifeboat clear of the parent ship. Their brief acceleration slammed Jason to the deck, then he floated as the boat went into free fall. The main-drive rockets didn't fire.

In that moment Jason learned what it was like to know he was dead. Without fuel the boat would drop into the jungle below, falling like a rock and blasting apart when it hit. There was no way out.

Then the rockets caught, roared, and he dropped to the deck, bruising his nose. He sat up, rubbing it and grinning. There was fuel in the tanks – the delay in starting had only been part of the launching cycle, giving the lifeboat time to fall clear of the ship. Now to get it under control. He pulled himself into the pilot's seat.

The altimeter had fed information to the auto-pilot, levelling the boat off parallel to the ground. Like all lifeboat controls these were childishly simple, designed to be used by novices in an emergency. The auto-pilot could not be shut off; it rode along with the manual controls, tempering foolish piloting. Jason hauled the control wheel into a tight turn and the auto-pilot gentled it to a soft curve.

Through the port, he could see the big ship blaring fire in a much tighter turn. Jason didn't know who was flying it or what they had in mind – he took no chances. Jamming the wheel forward into a dive, he cursed as they eased into a gentle drop. The larger ship had no such restrictions. It changed course with a violent manoeuvre and dived on him. The forward turret fired and an explosion at the stern rocked the little boat. This either knocked out the auto-pilot or shocked it into submission. The slow drop turned into a power dive and the jungle billowed up.

Jason pulled the wheel back into his gut and there was just time to get his arms in front of his face before they hit.

Thundering rockets and cracking trees ended in a great splash. Silence followed and the smoke drifted away. High above, the spaceship circled hesitantly. Dropping a bit as if wanting to go down and investigate. Then rising again as the urgent message for aid came from the city. Loyalty won and she turned and spewed fire towards home.

CHAPTER TWENTY-THREE

Tree branches had broken the lifeboat's fall, the bow rockets had burned out in emergency blast, and the swamp had cushioned the landing a bit. It was still a crash. The battered cylinder sank slowly into the stagnant water and thin mud of the swamp. The bow was well under before Jason managed to kick open the emergency hatch in the waist.

There was no way of knowing how long it would take for the boat to go under, and Jason was in no condition to ponder the situation. Battered and bloody, he had just enough drive left to get himself out. Wading and falling, he made his way to firmer land, sitting down heavily as soon as he found something that would support him.

Behind him, the lifeboat burbled and sank under the water. Bubbles of trapped air kept rising for a while, then stopped. The water stilled and, except for the broken branches and trees, there was no sign that a ship had ever come this way.

Insects whined across the swamp, and the only sound that broke the quiet of the woods beyond was the cruel scream of an animal pulling down its dinner. When that had echoed away in tiny waves of sound everything was silent.

Jason pulled himself out of the half trance with an effort. His body felt like it had been through a meat grinder, and it was almost impossible to think with the fog in his head. After minutes of deliberation, he figured out that the medikit was what he needed. The easy-off snap was very difficult and the button release didn't work. He finally twisted his arm around until it was under the orifice and pressed the entire unit down. It buzzed industriously; though he couldn't feel the needles, he guessed it had worked. His sight spun dizzily for a while, then cleared. Pain-killers went to work and he slowly came out of the dark cloud that had enveloped his brain since the crash.

Reason returned and loneliness rode along with it. He was without food, friendless, surrounded by the hostile forces of an alien planet. There was a rising panic that started deep inside of him, that took concentrated effort to hold down.

'Think Jason, don't emote.' He said it aloud to reassure himself, but was instantly sorry, because his voice sounded weak in the emptiness, with a ragged edge of hysteria to it. Something caught in his throat and he coughed to clear it, spitting out blood. Looking at the red stain, he was suddenly angry. Hating this deadly planet and the incredible stupidity of the people who lived on it. Cursing out loud was better and his voice didn't sound as weak now. He ended up shouting and shaking his fist at nothing in particular, but it helped. The anger washed away the fear and brought him back to reality.

Sitting on the ground felt good now. The sun was warm and when he leaned back he could almost forget the unending burden of doubled gravity. Anger had carried away fear, rest erased fatigue. From somewhere in the back of his mind, there popped up the old platitude: *Where there's life, there's hope.* He grimaced at the triteness of the words, at the same time realizing that a basic truth lurked there.

Count his assets. Well battered, but still alive. None of the bruises seemed very important, and no bones were broken. His gun was still working, it dipped in and out of the power holster as he thought about it. Pyrrans made rugged equipment. The medikit was operating as well. If he kept his senses, managed to walk in a fairly straight line and could live off the land, there was a fair chance he might make it back to the city. What kind of a reception would be waiting for him there was a different matter altogether. He would find that out after he arrived. Getting there had first priority.

On the debit side there stood the planet Pyrrus, strength-sapping gravity, murderous weather, and violent animals. Could he survive? As if to add emphasis to his thoughts, the sky darkened over and rain hissed into the forest, marching towards him. Jason scrambled to his feet and took a bearing before the rain closed down visibility. A jagged chain of mountains stood dimly on the horizons; he remembered crossing them on the flight out. They would do as a first goal. After he had reached them, he would worry about the next leg of the journey.

Leaves and dirt flew before the wind in quick gusts, then the rain washed over him. Soaked, chilled, already bone-tired, he pitted the tottering strength of his legs against the planet of death.

When nightfall came, it was still raining. There was no way of being sure of the direction, and no point in going on. If that wasn't enough, Jason was on the ragged edge of exhaustion. It was going to be a wet night. All the trees were thick-boled and slippery; he couldn't have climbed them on a one-G world.

The sheltered spots that he investigated, under fallen trees and beneath thick bushes, were just as wet as the rest of the forest. In the end he curled up on the leeward side of a tree, and fell asleep, shivering, with the water dripping off him.

The rain stopped around midnight and the temperature fell sharply. Jason woke sluggishly from a dream in which he was being frozen to death, to find it was almost true. Fine snow was sifting through the trees, powdering the ground and drifting against him. The cold bit into his flesh, and when he sneezed it hurt his chest. His aching and numb body only wanted rest, but the spark of reason that remained in him forced him to his feet. If he lay down now he would die. Holding one hand against the tree so he wouldn't fall, he began to trudge around it. Step after shuffling step, around and around, until the terrible cold eased a bit and he could stop shivering. Fatigue crawled up him like a muffling, grey blanket. He kept on walking, half the time with his eyes closed, opening them only when he fell and had to climb painfully to his feet again.

The sun burned away the snow clouds at dawn. Jason leaned against his tree and blinked up at the sky with sore eyes. The ground was white in all directions, except around the tree where his stumbling feet had churned a circle of black mud. His back against the smooth trunk, Jason sank slowly down to the ground, letting the sun soak into him.

Exhaustion had him light-headed, and his lips were cracked from thirst. Almost continuous coughing tore at his chest with fingers of fire. Though the sun was still low, it was hot already, burning his skin dry. Dry and hot.

It wasn't right. This thought kept nagging at his brain until he admitted it. Turned it over and over and looked at it from all sides. What wasn't right? The way he felt.

Pneumonia. He had all the symptoms.

His dry lips cracked and blood moistened them when he smiled. He had avoided all the animal perils of Pyrrus, all the big carnivores and poisonous reptiles, only to be laid low by the smallest beast of them all. Well, he had the remedy for this one too. Rolling up his sleeve with shaking fingers, he pressed the mouth of the medikit to his bare arm. It clicked and began to drone an angry whine. That meant something, he knew, but he just couldn't remember what. Holding it up he saw that one of the hypodermics was projecting half-way from its socket. Of course. It was empty of whatever antibiotic the analyser had called for. It needed refilling.

Jason hurled the thing away with a curse, and it splashed into a pool and was gone. End of medicine, end of medikit, end of Jason dinAlt. Single-handed battler against the perils of death-world. Strong-hearted stranger who could do as well as the natives. It had taken him all of one day on his own to get his death warrant signed.

A choking growl echoed behind him. He turned, dropped and fired in the same motion. It was all over before his conscious mind was aware it had happened. Pyrran training had conditioned his reflexes on the precortical level. Jason gaped at the ugly beast dying not a metre from him and realized he had been trained well.

His first reaction was unhappiness that he had killed one of the grubber dogs. When he looked closer he realized this animal was slightly different in markings, size and temper. Though most of its forequarters were blown away, blood pumping out in dying spurts, it kept trying to reach Jason. Before the eyes glazed with death, it had struggled its way almost to his feet.

It wasn't quite a grubber dog, though chances were it was a wild relative. Bearing the same relation as dog to wolf. He wondered if there were any other resemblances between wolves and this dead beast. Did they hunt in packs too?

As soon as the thought hit him he looked up – not a moment too soon. The great forms were drifting through the trees, closing in on him. When he shot two, the others snarled with rage and sank back into the forest. They didn't leave. Instead of being frightened by the deaths, they grew even more enraged.

Jason sat with his back to the tree and waited until they came close before he picked them off. With each shot and dying scream, the outraged survivors howled the louder. Some of them fought when they met, venting their rage. One stood on his hind legs and raked great strips of bark from a tree. Jason aimed a shot at it, but he was too far away to hit.

There were advantages to having a fever, he realized. Logically he knew he would live only to sunset, or until his gun was empty. Yet the fact didn't bother him greatly. Nothing really mattered. He slumped, relaxed completely, only raising his arm to fire, then letting it drop again. Every few minutes he had to move to look in the back of the tree, and kill any of them that were stalking him in the blind spot. He wished dimly that he were leaning against a smaller tree, but it wasn't worth the effort to go to one.

Some time in the afternoon, he fired his last shot. It killed an animal he had allowed to get close. He had noticed he was missing the longer shots. The beast snarled and dropped; the others that were close pulled back and howled in sympathy. One of them exposed himself and Jason pulled the trigger.

There was only a slight click. He tried again, in case it was just a misfire, but there was still only the click. The gun was empty, as was the spare clip pouch at his belt. There were vague memories of reloading, though he couldn't remember how many times he had done it.

This, then, was the end. They had all been right, Pyrrus was a match for him. Though they shouldn't talk. It would kill them all in the end too. Pyrrans never died in bed. Old Pyrrans never died, they just got et.

Now that he didn't have to force himself to stay alert and hold the gun, the fever took hold. He wanted to sleep and he knew it would be a long sleep. His eyes were almost closed as he watched the wary carnivores slip closer to him. The first one crept close enough to spring; he could see the muscles tensing in its leg.

It leaped. Whirling in mid-air and falling before it reached him. Blood ran from its gaping mouth and the short shaft of metal projected from the side of his head.

The two men walked out of the brush and looked down at him. Their mere presence seemed to have been enough for the carnivores, because they had all vanished.

Grubbers. He had been in such a hurry to reach the city that he had forgotten about the grubbers. It was good that they were here and Jason was very glad they had come. He couldn't talk very well, so he smiled to thank them. But this hurt his lips too much, so he went to sleep.

CHAPTER TWENTY-FOUR

For a strange length of time after that, there were only hazy patches of memory that impressed themselves on Jason. A sense of movement and large beasts around him. Walls, woodsmoke, the murmur of voices. None of it meant very much and he was too tired to care. It was easier and much better just to let go.

'About time,' Rhes said. 'A couple more days lying there like that and we would have buried you, even if you were still breathing.'

Jason blinked at him, trying to focus the face that swam above him. He finally recognized Rhes, and wanted to answer him. But talking only brought on a spell of body-wracking coughing. Someone held a cup to his lips and sweet fluid trickled down his throat. He rested, then tried again.

'How long have I been here?' The voice was thin and sounded far away. Jason had trouble recognizing it for his own.

'Eight days. And why didn't you listen when I talked to you?' Rhes said.

'You should have stayed near the ship when you crashed. Didn't you remember what I said about coming down anywhere on this continent? No matter, too late to worry about that. Next time listen to what I say. Our people moved fast and reached the site of the wreck before dark. They found the broken trees and the spot where the ship had sunk, and at first thought whoever had been in it had drowned. Then one of the dogs found your trail, but lost it again in the swamps during the night. They had a fine time with the mud and the snow and didn't have any luck at all in finding the spoor again. By the next afternoon they were ready to send for more help when they heard your firing. Just made it, from what I hear. Lucky one of them was a talker and could tell the wild dogs to clear out. Would have had to kill them all otherwise, and that's not healthy.'

'Thanks for saving my neck,' Jason said. 'That was closer than I like to come. What happened after? I was sure I was done for, I remember that much. Diagnosed all the symptoms of pneumonia. Guaranteed fatal in my condition without treatment. Looks like you were wrong when you said most of your remedies were useless – they seemed to work well on me.'

His voice died off as Rhes shook his head in a slow *no*, lines of worry sharp-cut into his face. Jason looked around and saw Naxa and another man. They had the same deeply unhappy expressions as Rhes.

'What is it?' Jason asked, feeling the trouble. 'If your remedies didn't work – what did? Not my medikit. That was empty. I remember losing it or throwing it away.'

'You were dying,' Rhes said slowly. 'We couldn't cure you. Only a junkman medicine machine could do that. We got one from the driver of the food truck.'

'But how?' Jason asked, dazed. 'You told me the city forbids you medicine. He wouldn't give you his own medikit. Not unless he was . . .'

Rhes nodded and finished the sentence. 'Dead. Of course he was dead. I killed him myself, with a great deal of pleasure.'

This hit Jason hard. He sagged against the pillows and thought of all those who had died since he had come to Pyrrus. The men who had died to save him, died so he could live, died because of his ideas. It was a burden of guilt that he couldn't bear to think about. Would it stop with Krannon – or would the city people try to avenge his death?

'Don't you realize what that means!' He gasped out the words. 'Krannon's death will turn the city against you. There'll be no more supplies. They'll attack you when they can, kill your people . . .'

'Of course we know that!' Rhes leaned forward, his voice hoarse and intense. 'It wasn't an easy decision to come to. We have always had a trading agreement with the junkmen. The trading trucks were inviolate. This was our last and only link to the galaxy outside the eventual hope of contacting them.'

'Yet you broke that link to save me – why?'

'Only you can answer that question completely. There was a great attack on the city and we saw their walls broken, they had to be moved back at one place. At the same time the space-ship was over the ocean, dropping bombs of some kind – the flash was reported. Then the ship returned and *you* left it in a smaller ship. They fired at you but didn't kill you. The little ship wasn't destroyed either; we are starting to raise it now. What does it all mean? We had no way of telling. We only knew it was something vitally important. You were alive, but would obviously die before you could talk. The small ship might be repaired to fly; perhaps that was your plan and that is why you stole it for us. We *couldn't* let you die, not even if it meant all-out war with the city. The situation was explained to all of our people who could be reached by screen and they voted to save you. I killed the junkman for his medicine, then rode two doryms to death to get here in time.

'Now tell us – what does it mean? What is your plan? How will it help us?'

Guilt leaned on Jason and stifled his mouth. A fragment of an ancient legend cut across his mind, about the Jona who wrecked the spacer so all in it died, yet he lived. Was that he? Had he wrecked a world? Could he dare admit to these people that he had taken the lifeboat only to save his own life?

The three Pyrrans leaned forward, waiting for his words. Jason closed his eyes so he wouldn't see their faces. What could he tell them? If he admitted the truth, they would undoubtedly kill him on the spot, considering it only justice. He wasn't fearful for his own life any more, but if he died the other deaths would all have been in vain. And there still was a way to end this planetary war. All the facts were available now, it was just a matter of putting them together. If only he wasn't so tired, he would see the solution. It was right there, lurking around a corner in his brain, waiting to be dragged out.

There was the sudden sound of heavy feet stamping outside the cabin, and a man's muffled shouting. No one except Jason seemed to notice. They were too intent on his answer. He groped in his mind, but couldn't find words to explain. What-ever he did, he couldn't admit the truth now. If he died all hope died. He had to lie to gain time, then find the correct solution that seemed so tantalizingly near. Yet he was too tired even to phrase a plausible lie.

The sound of the door bursting open crashed through the stillness of the room. A gnarled, stubby man stood there, his anger-red face set off by a full white beard.

'Everyone deaf?' he snarled. 'I ride all night and shout my lungs out and you just squat here like a bunch a' egg-hatching birds. Get out! Quake! A big quake on the way!'

They were all standing now, shouting questions. Rhes's voice cut through the uproar. 'Hananas! How much time do we have?'

'Time! Who knows about time!' the greybeard cursed. 'Get out or you're dead, s'all I know.'

No one stopped to argue now. There was a furious rush and within a minute Jason was being strapped into a litter on one of the doryms. 'What's happening?' he asked the man who was tying him into place.

'Earthquake coming,' he answered, his fingers busy with the knots. 'Hananas is the best quakeman we have. He always knows before a quake is going to happen. If the word can be passed quick enough we get away. Quakemen always know, say they can feel them coming.' He jerked the last knot tight and was gone.

Night came as they were starting, the red of sunset matched by a surly scarlet glow in the northern sky. There was a distant rumbling, more felt than heard, and the ground stirred underfoot. The doryms hurried into a shambling run without being prodded. They splashed through a swamp and on the other side Hananas changed their course abruptly. A little later, when the southern sky exploded, Jason knew why. Flames lit the scene brightly, ashes sifted down and hot lumps of rock crashed into the trees. They steamed when they hit, and if it hadn't been for the earlier rain they would have been faced with a forest fire as well.

Something large loomed up next to the line of march, and when they crossed an open space Jason looked at it in the reflected light from the sky.

'Rhes –' he choked, pointing. Rhes, riding next to him, looked at the great beast, shaggy body and twisted horns as high as their shoulders, then looked away. He wasn't frightened or apparently even interested. Jason looked around then and began to understand.

All of the fleeing animals made no sound, that's why he hadn't noticed them before. But on both sides dark forms ran between the trees. Some he recognized, most of them he didn't. For a few minutes a pack of wild dogs ran near them, even mingling with the domesticated dogs. No notice was taken. Flying things flapped by overhead. Under the greater threat of the volcanoes all other battles were forgotten. Life respected life. A herd of fat, pig-like beasts with curling tusks blundered through the line. The doryms slowed, picking their steps carefully so they wouldn't step on them. Smaller animals sometimes clung to the backs of the bigger ones, riding untouched a while, before they leaped off.

Pounded mercilessly by the jarring litter, Jason fell wearily into a light sleep. It was shot through with dreams of the rushing animals, hurrying on for ever in silence. With his eyes open or shut, he saw the same endless stream of beasts.

It all meant something and he frowned as he tried to think what. Animals running, Pyrran animals.

He sat bolt upright suddenly, twisting in his litter, wide awake and staring down in comprehension.

'What is it?' Rhes asked, swinging his dorym in close.

'Go on,' Jason said. 'Get us out of this, and get us out safely. I know how your people can get what they want, end the war now. There *is* a way, and I know how it can be done.'

CHAPTER TWENTY-FIVE

There were few coherent memories of the ride. Some things stood out sharply like the space-ship-sized lump of burning scoria that had plunged into a lake near them, showering the line with hot drops of water. But mostly it was just a seemingly endless ride, with Jason still too weak to care much about it. By dawn the danger area was behind them and the march had slowed to a walk. The animals had vanished as the quake was left behind, going their own ways, still in silent armistice.

The peace of mutually shared danger was over; Jason found that out when they stopped to rest and eat. He and Rhes went to sit on the soft grass, near a fallen tree. A wild dog had arrived there first. It lay under the log, muscles tensed, the ruddy morning light striking a red glint from its eyes. Rhes faced it, not three metres away, without moving a muscle. He made no attempt to reach one of his weapons or to call for help. Jason stood still as well, hoping the Pyrran knew what he was doing.

With no warning at all the dog sprang straight at them. Jason fell backward as Rhes pushed him aside. The Pyrran dropped at the same time – only now his hand held the long knife, yanked from the sheath strapped to his thigh. With unseen speed the knife came up, the dog twisted in mid-air, trying to bite it. Instead it sank in behind the dog's forelegs, the beast's own weight tearing a deadly gaping wound the length of its body. It was still alive when it hit the ground, but Rhes was astraddle it, pulling back the bony-plated head to cut the soft throat underneath.

The Pyrran carefully cleaned his knife on the dead animal's fur, then returned it to the sheath. 'They're usually no trouble,' he said quietly, 'but it was excited. Probably lost the rest of the pack in the quake.' His actions were the direct opposite of the city Pyrrans. He had not looked for trouble nor started the fight. Instead he had avoided it as long as he could. But when the beast charged, it had been neatly and efficiently dispatched. Now, instead of gloating over his victory, he seemed troubled over an unnecessary death.

It made sense. Everything on Pyrrus made sense. Now he knew how the deadly planetary battle had started – and he knew how it could be ended. All the deaths had *not* been in vain. Each one had helped him along the road a little more towards the final destination. There was just one final thing to be done.

Rhes was watching him now and he knew they shared the same thoughts. 'Explain yourself,' Rhes said. 'What did you mean when you said we could wipe out the junkmen and get our freedom?'

Jason didn't bother to correct the misquote; it was best they considered him a hundred per cent on their side.

'Get the others together and I'll tell you. I particularly want to see Naxa and any other talkers who are here.'

They gathered quickly when the word was passed. All of them knew that the junkman had been killed to save this off-worlder, that their hope of salvation lay with him. Jason looked at the crowd of faces turned towards him and reached for the right words to tell them what had to be done. It didn't help to know that many of them would be killed doing it.

'We all want to see an end to the war here on Pyrrus. There is a way, but it will cost human lives. Some of you may die doing it. I think the price is worth it, because success will bring you everything you have ever wanted.' He looked around at the tense, waiting circle.

'We are going to invade the city, break through the perimeter. I know how it can be done. . . .'

A mutter of sound spread across the crowd. Some of them looked excited, happy with the thought of killing their hereditary enemies. Others stared at Jason as if he were mad. A few were dazed at the magnitude of the thought, this carrying of the battle to the stronghold of the heavily armed enemy. They quieted when Jason raised his hand.

'I know it sounds impossible,' he said. 'But let me explain. Something must be done – and now is the time to do it. The situation can only get worse from now on. The city Pyrr . . . the junkmen can get along without your food, their concentrates taste awful but they sustain life. But they are going to turn against you in every way they can. No more metals for your tools or replacements for your electronic equipment. Their hatred will probably make them seek out your farms and destroy them from the ship. All of this won't be comfortable – and there will be worse to come. In the city they are losing their war against this planet. Each year there are less of them, and some day they will all be dead. Knowing how they feel, I am sure they will destroy their ship first, and the entire planet as well, if that is possible.'

'How can we stop them?' someone called out.

'By hitting *now*,' Jason answered. 'I know all the details of the city and I know how the defences are set up. Their perimeter is designed to protect them from animal life, but we could break through it if we were really determined.'

'What good would that do?' Rhes snapped. 'We crack the perimeter and they draw back – then counter-attack in force. How can we stand against their weapons?'

'We won't have to. Their space-port touches the perimeter, and I know the exact spot where the ship stands. That is the place where we will break through. There is no formal guard on the ship and only a few people in the area. We will capture the ship. Whether we can fly it or not is unimportant. Who controls the ship controls Pyrrus. Once there we threaten to destroy it if they don't meet our terms. They have the choice of mass suicide or cooperation. I hope they have the brains to cooperate.'

His words shocked them into silence for an instant, then they surged into a wave of sound. There was no agreement, just excitement, and Rhes finally brought them to order.

'Quiet!' he shouted. 'Wait until Jason finishes before you decide. We still haven't heard how this proposed invasion is to be accomplished.'

'The plan I have depends on the talkers,' Jason said. 'Is Naxa there?' He waited until the fur-wrapped man had pushed to the front. 'I want to know more about the talkers, Naxa. I know you can speak to doryms and the dogs here – but what about the wild animals? Can you make them do what you want?'

'They're animals – course we can talk t' them. Th' more talkers, th' more power. Make 'em do just what we want.'

'Then the attack will work,' Jason said excitedly. 'Could you get your talkers all on one side of the city – the opposite side from the spaceport – and stir the animals up? Make them attack the perimeter?'

'Could we!' Naxa shouted, carried away by the idea. 'We'd bring in animals from all over, start th' biggest attack they ev'r saw!'

'Then that's it. Your talkers will launch the attack on the far side of the perimeter. If you keep out of sight, the guards will have no idea that it is anything more than an animal attack. I've seen how they work. As an attack mounts, they call for reserves inside the city and drain men away from the other parts of the perimeter. At the height of the battle, when they have all their forces committed across the city, I'll lead the attack that will break through and capture the ship. That's the plan and it's going to work.'

Jason sat down then, half fell down, drained of strength. He lay and listened as the debate went back and forth, Rhes ordering it and keeping it going. Difficulties were raised and eliminated. No one could find a basic fault with the plan. There were plenty of flaws in it, things that might go wrong, but Jason didn't mention them. These people wanted his idea to work and they were going to make it work.

It finally broke up and they moved away. Rhes came over to Jason.

'The basics are settled,' he said. 'All here are in agreement. They are spreading the word by messenger to all the talkers. The talkers are the heart of the attack, and the more we have, the better it will go off. We don't dare use the screens to call them; there is a good chance that the junkmen can intercept our messages. It will take five days before we are ready to go ahead.'

'I'll need all that time if I'm to be any good,' Jason said. 'Now let's get some rest.'

CHAPTER TWENTY-SIX

'It's a strange feeling,' Jason said. 'I've never really seen the perimeter from this side before. Ugly is about the only word for it.'

He lay on his stomach next to Rhes, looking through a screen of leaves, downhill towards the perimeter. They were both wrapped in heavy furs, in spite of the midday heat, with thick leggings and leather gauntlets to protect their hands. The gravity and the heat were already making Jason dizzy, but he forced himself to ignore this.

Ahead, on the far side of a burnt corridor, stood the perimeter. A high wall, of varying height and texture, seemingly made of all the odds and ends in the world. It was impossible to tell what it had originally been constructed of. Generations of attackers had bruised, broken, and undermined it. Repairs had been quickly made, patches thrust roughly into place and fixed there. Crude masonry crumbled and gave way to a rat's nest of woven timbers. This overlapped a length of pitted metal, large plates riveted together. Even this metal had been eaten through and bursting sandbags spilled out of a jagged hole. Over the surface of the wall detector wires and charged cables looped and hung. At odd intervals automatic flame-throwers thrust their nozzles over the parapet above and swept the base of the wall clear of any life that might have come close.

'Those flame things can cause us trouble,' Rhes said. 'That one covers the area where you want to break in.'

'It'll be no problem,' Jason assured him. 'It may look like it is firing a random pattern, but it's really not. It varies a simple sweep just enough to fool an animal, but was never meant to keep men out. Look for yourself. It fires at regularly repeated two-, four-, three- and one-minute intervals.'

They crawled back to the hollow where Naxa and the others waited for them. There were only thirty men in the party. What they had to do could only be done with a fast, light force. Their strongest weapon was surprise. Once that was gone their other weapons wouldn't hold out for seconds against the city guns. Everyone looked uncomfortable in the fur and leather wrappings, and some of the men had loosened them to cool off.

'Wrap up,' Jason ordered. 'None of you have been this close to the perimeter before and you don't understand how deadly it is here. Naxa is keeping the larger animals away and you all can handle the smaller ones. That isn't the danger. Every thorn is poisoned, and even the blades of grass carry a deadly sting. Watch out for insects of any kind and once we start moving breathe only through the wet cloths.'

'He's right,' Naxa snorted. 'N'ver been closer 'n this m'self. Death, death up by that wall. Do like 'e says.'

They could only wait then, honing down already needle-sharp crossbow bolts, and glancing up at the slowly moving sun. Only Naxa didn't share the unrest. He sat, eyes unfocused, feeling the movement of animal life in the jungle around them.

'On the way,' he said. 'Biggest thing I 'ver heard. Not a beast 'tween here and the mountains ain't howlin' 'is lungs out, runnin' towards the city.'

Jason was aware of part of it. A tension in the air and a wave of intensified anger and hatred. It would work, he knew, if they could only keep the attack confined to a small area. The talkers had seemed sure of it. They had stalked out quietly that morning, a thin line of ragged men, moving in a mental sweep that would round up the Pyrran life and send it charging against the city.

'They hit!' Naxa said suddenly.

The men were on their feet now, staring in the direction of the city. Jason had felt the twist in his gut as the attack had been driven home, and knew that this was it. There was the sound of shots and a heavy booming far away. Thin streamers of smoke began to blow above the tree-tops.

'Let's get into position,' Rhes said.

Around them the jungle howled with an echo of hatred. The half-sentient plants writhed and the air was thick with small flying things. Naxa sweated and mumbled as he turned back the animals that crashed towards them. By the time they reached the last screen of foliage before the burned-out area, they had lost four men. One had been stung by an insect; Jason got the medikit to him in time but he was so sick he had to turn back. The other three were bitten or scratched and treatment came too late. Their swollen, twisted bodies were left behind on the trail.

'Dam' beasts hurt m' head,' Naxa muttered. 'When we go in?'

'Not yet,' Rhes said. 'We wait for the signal.'

One of the men carried the radio. He set it down carefully, then threw the aerial over a branch. The set was shielded, so no radiation leaked out to give them away. It was turned on, but only a hiss of atmospheric static came from the speaker.

'We could have timed it . . .' Rhes said.

'No, we couldn't,' Jason told him. 'Not accurately. We want to hit that wall at the height of the attack, when our chances are best. Even if they hear the message it won't mean a thing to them inside. And a few minutes later it won't matter.'

The sound from the speaker changed. A voice spoke a short sentence, then cut off.

'Bring me three barrels of flour.'

'Let's go,' Rhes urged as he started forward.

'Wait,' Jason said, taking him by the arm. 'I'm timing the flamethrower. It's due in . . . *there*!' A blast of fire sprayed the ground, then turned off. 'We have four minutes to the next one – we hit the long period!'

They ran, stumbling in the soft ashes, tripping over charred bones and rusted metal. Two men grabbed Jason under the arm and half-carried him across the ground. It hadn't been planned that way, but it saved precious seconds. They dropped him against the wall and he fumbled out the bombs he had made. The charges from Krannon's gun, taken when he was killed, had been hooked together with a firing circuit. All the moves had been rehearsed carefully and they went smoothly now.

Jason had picked the metal wall as being the best spot to break in. It offered the most resistance to the native life, so the chances were it wouldn't be reinforced with sandbags or fill, the way other parts of the wall were. If he was wrong, they were all dead.

The first men had slapped their wads of sticky congealed sap against the wall. Jason pressed the charges into them and they stuck, a roughly rectangular pattern as high as a man. While he did this, the detonating wire was run out to its length and the raiders pressed back against the base of the wall. Jason stumbled through the ashes to the detonator, fell on it and pressed the switch at the same time.

Behind him a thundering bang shook the wall and red flame burst out. Rhes was the first one there, pulling at the twisted and smoking metal with his gloved hands. Others grabbed on and bent the jagged pieces aside. The hole was filled with smoke and nothing was visible through it. Jason dived into the opening, rolled on a heap of rubble and smacked into something solid. When he blinked the smoke from his eyes, he looked around him.

He was inside the city.

The others poured through now, picking him up as they charged in so that he wouldn't be trampled underfoot. Someone spotted the spaceship and they ran that way.

A man ran around the corner of a building towards them. His Pyrran reflexes sent him springing into the safety of a doorway the same moment he saw the invaders. But they were Pyrrans too. The man slumped slowly back on to the street, three metal bolts sticking out of his body. They ran on without stopping, running between the low storehouses. The ship stood ahead.

Someone had reached it before them; they could see the outer hatch slowly grinding shut. A hail of bolts from the bows crashed into it with no effect.

'Keep going!' Jason shouted. 'Get next to the hull before he reaches the guns.'

This time three men didn't make it. The rest of them were under the belly of the ship when every gun let go at once. Most of them were aimed away from the ship, still the scream of shells and electric discharges were earshattering. The three men still in the open dissolved under the fire. Whoever was inside the ship had hit all the gun trips at once, both to knock out the attackers and summon aid. He would be on the screen now, calling for help. Their time was running out.

Jason reached up and tried to open the hatch, while the others watched. It was locked from the inside. One of the men brushed him aside and pulled at the inset handle. It broke off in his hand but the hatch remained closed.

The big guns had stopped now and they could hear again.

'Did anyone get the gun from that dead man?' he asked. 'It would blow this thing open.'

'No,' Rhes said, 'we didn't stop.'

Before the words were out of his mouth, two men were running back towards the building, angling away from each other. The ship's guns roared again, a string of explosions cut across one man. Before they could change direction and find the other man he had reached the buildings.

He returned quickly, darting into the open to throw the gun to them. Before he could dive back to safety, the shells caught him.

Jason grabbed up the gun as it skidded almost to his feet. They heard the sound of wide open truck turbines screaming towards them as he blasted the lock. The mechanism sighed and the hatch sagged open. They were all through the airlock before the first truck appeared. Naxa stayed behind with the gun, to hold the lock until they could take the control room.

Everyone climbed faster than Jason, once he had pointed them the way, so the battle was over when he got there. The single city Pyrran looked like a pincushion. One of the techs had found the gun controls and was shooting wildly, the sheer quantity of his fire driving the trucks back.

'Someone get on the radio and tell the talkers to call the attack off,' Jason said. He found the communications screen and snapped it on. Kerk's wide-eyed face stared at him from the screen.

'*You!*' Kerk said, breathing the word like a curse.

'Yes, it's me,' Jason answered. He talked without looking up, while his hands were busy at the control board. 'Listen to me, Kerk – and don't doubt anything I say. I may not know how to fly one of these ships, but I do know how to blow them up. Do you hear that sound?' He flipped over a switch and the far-away whine of a pump droned faintly. 'That's the main fuel pump. If I let it run – which I won't right now – it could quickly fill the drive chamber with raw fuel. Pour in so much that it would run out of the stern tubes. Then what do you think would happen to your one-and-only spacer if I pressed the firing button? I'm not asking you what would happen to me – since you don't care – but you need this ship the way you need life itself.'

There was only silence in the cabin now. The men who had won the ship turned to face him. Kerk's voice grated loudly through the room.

'What do you want, Jason? What are you trying to do? Why did you lead those animals in here?' His voice cracked and broke as anger choked him and spilled over.

'Watch your tongue, Kerk,' Jason said with soft menace. 'These *men* you are talking about are the only ones on Pyrrus who have a spaceship. If you want them to share it with you, you had better learn to talk nicely. Now come over here at once – and bring Brucco and Meta.' Jason looked at the older man's florid and swollen face and felt a measure of sympathy. 'Don't look so unhappy, it's not the end of the world. In fact, it might be the beginning of one. And another thing, leave this channel open when you go. Have it hooked into every screen in the city, so everyone can see what happens here. Make sure it's taped too, for replay.'

Kerk started to say something, but changed his mind before he did. He left the screen, but the set stayed alive. Carrying the scene in the control room to the entire city.

CHAPTER TWENTY-SEVEN

The fight was over. It had ended so quickly the fact hadn't really sunk in yet. Rhes rubbed his hand against the gleaming metal of the control console, letting the reality of touch convince him. The other men milled about, looking out through the viewscreens or soaking in the mechanical strangeness of the room.

Jason was physically exhausted, but he couldn't let it show. He opened the pilot's med-box and dug through it until he found the stimulants. Three of the little gold pills washed the fatigue from his body, and he could think clearly again.

'Listen to me,' he shouted. 'The fight's not over yet. They'll try anything to take this ship back and we have to be ready. I want one of the techs to go over these boards until he finds the lock controls. Make sure all the airlocks and ports are sealed. Send men to check them, if necessary. Turn on all the screens to scan in every direction, so that no one can get near the ship. We'll need a guard in the engine room; my control could be cut if they broke in there. And there had better be a room-by-room search of the ship, in case someone else is locked in with us.'

The men had something to do now and felt relieved. Rhes split them up into groups and set them to work. Jason stayed at the controls, his hand next to the pump switch. The battle wasn't over yet.

'There's a truck coming,' Rhes called, 'going slow.'

'Should I blast it?' the man at the gun controls asked.

'Hold your fire,' Jason said, 'until we can see who it is. If it's the people I sent for, let them through.'

As the truck came on slowly, the gunner tracked it with his sights. There was a driver and three passengers. Jason waited until he was positive who they were.

'Those are the ones,' he said. 'Stop them at the lock, Rhes, make them come in one at a time. Take their guns as they enter, then strip them of *all* their equipment. There is no way of telling what could be a concealed weapon. Be specially careful of Brucco – he's the thin one with a face like an axe edge – make sure you strip him clean. He's a specialist in weapons and survival. And bring the driver, too; we don't want him reporting back about the broken airlock or the state of our guns.'

Waiting was hard. His hand stayed next to the pump switch, even though he knew he could never use it. Just as long as the others thought he would.

There were stampings and muttered curses in the corridor; the prisoners were pushed in. Jason had one look at their deadly expressions and clenched fists before he called to Rhes.

'Keep them against the wall and watch them. Bowmen, keep your weapons up.' He looked at the people who had once been his friends and who now swam in hatred for him. Meta, Kerk, Brucco. The driver was Skop, the man Kerk had once appointed to guard him. He looked ready to explode now that the roles had been reversed.

'Pay close attention,' Jason said. 'because your lives depend upon it. Keep your backs to the wall and don't attempt to come any closer to me than you are now. If you do, you will be shot instantly. If we were alone, any one of you could undoubtedly reach me before I threw this switch. But we're not. You have Pyrran reflexes and muscles – but so do the bowmen. Don't gamble. Because it won't be a gamble. It will be suicide. I'm telling you this for your own protection. So we can talk peacefully without one of you losing his temper and suddenly getting shot. *There is no way out of this.* You are going to be forced to listen to everything I say. You can't escape or kill me. The war is over.'

'And we lost – and all because of you, you *traitor*!' Meta snarled.

'Wrong on both counts,' Jason said blandly. 'I'm not a traitor because I owe my allegiance to all men on this planet, both inside the perimeter and out. I never pretended differently. As to losing, why, you haven't lost anything. In fact you've won. Won your war against this planet, if you will only hear me out.' He turned to Rhes, who was frowning in angry puzzlement. 'Of course your people have won also, Rhes. No more war with the city, you'll get medicine, off-planet contact, everything you want.'

'Pardon me for being cynical,' Rhes said. 'But you're promising the best of all possible worlds for everyone. That will be a little hard to deliver when our interests are opposed so.'

'You strike through to the heart of the matter,' Jason said. 'Thank you. This mess will be settled by seeing that everyone's interests are not opposed. Peace between the city and farms, with an end to the useless war you have been fighting. Peace between mankind and the Pyrran life forms – because that particular war is at the bottom of all your troubles.'

'The man's mad,' Kerk said.

'Perhaps. You'll judge that after you hear me out. I'm going to tell you the history of this planet, because that is where both the trouble and the solution lie.

'When the settlers landed on Pyrrus three hundred years ago, they missed the one important thing about this planet, the factor that makes it different from any other planet in the galaxy. They can't be blamed for the oversight, they had enough other things to worry about. The gravity was about the only thing familiar to them, the rest of the environment was a shocking change from the climate-controlled industrial world they had left. Storms, volcanism, floods, earthquakes – it was enough to drive them insane, and I'm sure many of them did go mad. The animal and insect life was a constant annoyance, nothing at all like the few harmless and protected species they had known. I'm sure they never realized that the Pyrran life was telepathic as well –'

'That again!' Brucco snapped. 'True or not, it is of no importance. I was tempted to agree with your theory of *psi*onic controlled attack on us, but the deadly fiasco you staged proved that theory wrong.'

'I agree,' Jason answered. 'I was completely mistaken when I thought some outside agency directed the attack on the city with *psi*onic control. It seemed a logical theory at the time and the evidence pointed that way. The expedition to the island *was* a deadly fiasco – only don't forget that attack was the direct opposite of what I wanted to have done. If I had gone into the cave myself, none of the deaths would have been necessary. I think it would have been discovered that the plant creatures were nothing more than an advanced life form with unusual *psi* ability. They simply resonated strongly to the *psi*onic attack on the city. I had the idea backward thinking they instigated the battle. We'll never know the truth, though, because they are destroyed. But their deaths did do one thing. Showed us where to find the real culprits, the creatures who are leading, directing and inspiring the war against the city.'

'*Who?*' Kerk breathed the question, rather than spoke it.

'Why, *you*, of course,' Jason told him. 'Not you alone, but all of your people in the city. Perhaps you don't like this war. However, you are responsible for it and keep it going.'

Jason had to force back a smile as he looked at their dumbfounded expression. He also had to prove his point quickly, before even his allies began to think him insane.

'Here is how it works. I said Pyrran life was telepathic – and I meant all life. Every single insect, plant and animal. At one time in this planet's violent history, these *psi*onic mutations proved to be survival types. They existed when other species died, and in the end I'm sure they cooperated in wiping out the last survivors of the non-*psi* strains. Cooperation is the key word here. Because while they still competed against each other under normal conditions, they worked together against anything that threatened them as a whole. When a natural upheaval or a tidal wave threatened them, they fled from it in harmony. You can see a milder form of this same behaviour on any planet that is subject to forest fires. But here, mutual survival was carried to an extreme because of the violent conditions. Perhaps some of the life forms even developed precognition like the human quakemen. With this advance warning, the larger beasts fled. The smaller ones developed seeds, or burrs or eggs, that could be carried to safety by the wind or in the animals' fur, thus insuring racial survival. I know this is true because I watched it myself when we were escaping a quake.'

'Admitted – all your points admitted,' Brucco shouted. 'But what does it have to do with *us*? So all the animals run away together, what does that have to do with the war?'

'They do more than run away together,' Jason told him. 'They work together against any natural disaster that threatens them all. Some day, I'm sure, ecologists will go into raptures over the complex adjustments that occur here in the advent of blizzards, floods, fires and other disasters. There is only one reaction we really care about now, though. That's the one directed towards the city people. Don't you realize yet – they treat you all as another natural disaster!

'We'll never know exactly how it came about, though there is a clue in that diary I found, dating from the first days on this planet. It said that a forest fire seemed to have driven new species towards the settlers. Those weren't new beasts at all – just old ones with new attitudes. Can't you just imagine how those protected, over-civilized settlers acted when faced with a forest fire? They panicked, of course. If the settlers were in the path of the fire, the animals must have rushed right through their camp. Their reaction would undoubtedly have been to shoot the fleeing creatures down.

'When they did that, they classified themselves as a natural disaster. Disasters take any form. Bipeds with guns could easily be included in the category. The Pyrran animals attacked, were shot, and the war began. The survivors kept attacking and informed all the life forms what the fight was about. The radioactivity of this planet must cause plenty of mutations – and the favourable, survival mutation was now one that was deadly to man. I'll hazard a guess that the *psi* function even instigates mutations, some of the deadlier types are just too one-sided to have come about naturally in a brief three hundred years.

'The settlers of course fought back, and kept their status as a natural disaster intact. Through the centuries, they improved their killing methods, not that it did the slightest good, as you know. You city people, their descendants, are heirs to this heritage of hatred. You fight and are slowly being defeated. How can you possibly win against the biological reserves of a planet that can re-create itself each time to meet any new attack?'

Silence followed Jason's words. Kerk and Meta stood white-faced as the impact of the disclosure sunk in. Brucco mumbled and checked points off on his fingers, searching for weak spots in the chain of reasoning. The fourth city Pyrran, Skop, ignored all these foolish words that he couldn't understand – or did not want to understand – and would have killed Jason in an instant if there had been the slightest chance of success.

It was Rhes who broke the silence. His quick mind had taken in the factors and sorted them out. 'There's one thing wrong,' he said. 'What about us? We live on the surface of Pyrrus without perimeters or guns. Why aren't we attacked as well? We're human, descended from the same people as the junkmen.'

'You're not attacked,' Jason told him, 'because you don't identify yourself as a natural disaster. Animals can live on the slopes of a dormant volcano, fighting and dying in natural competition. But they'll flee together when the volcano erupts. That eruption is what makes the mountain a natural disaster. In the case of human beings, it is their thoughts that identify them as life form or disaster. Mountain or volcano. In the city everyone radiates suspicion and death. They enjoy killing, thinking about killing, and planning for killing. This is natural selection too, you realize. These are the survival traits that work best in the city. Outside the city, men think differently. If they are threatened individually, they fight, as will any other creature. Under more general survival threats, they cooperate completely with the rules for universal survival that the city people break.'

'How did it begin – this separation, I mean, between the two groups?' Rhes asked.

'We'll probably never know,' Jason said. 'I think your people must have originally been farmers, or *psi*onic sensitives who were not with the others during some natural disaster. They would of course act correctly by Pyrran standards, and survive. This would cause a difference of opinion with the city people who saw killing as the answer. It's obvious, whatever the reason, that two separate communities were established early, and soon separated except for the limited amount of barter that benefited both.'

'I still can't believe it,' Kerk mumbled. 'It makes a terrible kind of truth, every step of the way, but I still find it hard to accept. There *must* be another explanation.'

Jason shook his head slowly. 'None. This is the only one that works. We've eliminated the other ones, remember? I can't blame you for finding it hard to believe, since it is in direct opposition to everything you've understood to be true in the past. It's like altering a natural law. As if I gave you proof that gravity didn't really exist, that it was a force altogether different from the immutable one we know, one you could get around when you understood how. You'd want more proof than words. Probably want to see someone walking on air.'

'Which isn't such a bad idea at that,' he added, turning to Naxa. 'Do you hear any animals around the ship now? Not the ones you're used to, but the mutated, violent kind that live only to attack the city.'

'Place's crawling with 'em,' Naxa said. 'Just lookin' for somethin' t' kill.'

'Could you capture one?' Jason asked. 'Without getting yourself killed, I mean?'

Naxa snorted contempt as he turned to leave. 'Beast's not born yet that'll hurt me.'

They stood quietly, each one wrapped tightly around by his own thoughts, while they waited for Naxa to return. Jason had nothing more to say. He would do one more thing to try and convince them of the facts; after that it would be up to each of them to reach a conclusion.

The talker returned quickly with a stingwing tied by one leg to a length of leather. It flapped and shrieked and he carried it in.

'In the middle of the room, away from everybody,' Jason told him. 'Can you get that beast to sit on something and not flap around?'

'My hand good enough?' he asked, flipping the creature up so that it clung to the back of his gauntlet. 'That's how I caught it.'

'Does anyone doubt that this is a real stingwing?' Jason asked. 'I want to make sure you all believe there is no trickery here.'

'The thing is real,' Brucco said. 'I can smell the poison in the wing claws from here.' He pointed to the dark marks on the leather where the liquid had dripped. 'If that eats through the glove, he's a dead man.'

'Then we agree it's real,' Jason said. 'Real and deadly, and the only test of the theory will be if you people from the city can approach it like Naxa here.'

They drew back automatically when he said it. Because they knew that stingwing was synonymous with death. Past, present and future. You don't change a natural law. Meta spoke for all of them.

'We – can't. This man lives in the jungle, like an animal himself. Somehow he's learned to get near them. But you can't expect us to.'

Jason spoke quickly, before the talker could react to the insult. 'Of course I expect you to. That's the whole idea. If you don't hate the beast and expect it to attack you – why, it won't. Think of it as a creature from a different planet, something harmless.'

'I can't,' she said. 'It's a *stingwing*!'

As they talked, Brucco stepped forward, his eyes fixed steadily on the creature perched on the glove. Jason signalled the bowmen to hold their fire. Brucco stopped at a safe distance and kept looking steadily at the stingwing. It rustled its leathery wings uneasily and hissed. A drop of poison formed at the tip of each great poison claw on its wings. The control room was filled with a deadly silence.

Slowly he raised his hand. Carefully putting it out, over the animal. The hand dropped a little, rubbed the stingwing's head once, then fell back to his side. The animal did nothing except stir slightly under the touch.

There was a concerted sigh, as those who had been unknowingly holding their breath breathed again.

'How did you do it?' Meta asked in a hushed voice.

'Hmmm, what?' Brucco said, apparently snapping out of a daze. 'Oh, touching the thing. Simple, really, I just pretended it was one of the training aids I use, a realistic and harmless duplicate. I kept my mind on that single thought and it worked.' He looked down at his hand, then back to the sting-wing. His voice was quieter now, as if he spoke from a distance. 'It's not a training aid, you know. It's real. Deadly. The off-worlder is right. He's right about everything he said.'

With Brucco's success as an example, Kerk came close to the animal. He walked stiffly, as if on the way to his execution, and runnels of sweat poured down his rigid face But he believed and kept his thoughts directed away from the stingwing and he could touch it unharmed.

Meta tried but couldn't fight down the horror it raised when she came close. 'I am trying,' she said, 'and I do believe you now – but I just can't do it.'

Skop screamed when they all looked at him, shouted it was all a trick, and had to be clubbed unconscious when he attacked the bowmen.

Understanding had come to Pyrrus.

CHAPTER TWENTY-EIGHT

'What do we do now?' Meta asked. Her voice was troubled, questioning. She voiced the thoughts of all the Pyrrans in the room, and the thousands who watched on their screens.

'What will we do?' They turned to Jason, waiting for an answer. For the moment their differences were forgotten. The people from the city were staring expectantly at him, as were the crossbowmen with half-lowered weapons. This stranger had confused and changed the old world they had known, and presented them with a newer and stranger one, with alien problems.

'Hold on,' he said, raising his hand. 'I'm no doctor of social ills. I'm not going to try and cure this planet full of musclebound sharpshooters. I've just squeezed through up to now, and by the law of averages I should be ten times dead.'

'Even if all you say is true, Jasno,' Meta said, 'you are still the only person who can help us. What will the future be like?'

Suddenly weary, Jason slumped into the pilot's chair. He glanced around at the circle of people. They seemed sincere. None of them even appeared to have noticed that he no longer had his hand on the pump switch. For the moment, at least, the war between city and country was forgotten.

'I'll give you my conclusions,' Jason said, twisting in the chair, trying to find a comfortable position for his aching bones. 'I've been doing a lot of thinking the last day or two, searching for the answer. The very first thing I realized was that the perfect and logical solution wouldn't do at all. I'm afraid the old ideal of the lion lying down with the lamb doesn't work out in practice. About all it does is make a fast lunch for the lion. Ideally, now that you all know the real cause of your trouble, you should tear down the perimeter and have the city and forest people mingled in brotherly love. Makes just as pretty a picture as the one of lion and lamb. And would undoubtedly have the same result. Someone would remember how really filthy the grubbers are, or how stupid junkmen can be, and there would be a fresh corpse cooling. The fight would spread and the victors would be eaten by the wildlife that swarmed over the undefended perimeter. No, the answer isn't that easy.'

As the Pyrrans listened to him, they realized where they were and glanced around uneasily. The guards raised their crossbows again and the prisoners stepped back to the wall and looked surly.

'See what I mean?' Jason asked. 'Didn't take long, did it?' They all looked a little sheepish at their unthinking reactions.

'If we're going to find a decent plan for the future, we'll have to take inertia into consideration. Mental inertia, for one. Just because you know a thing is true in theory doesn't make it true in fact. The barbaric religions of primitive worlds hold not a germ of scientific fact, though they claim to explain all. Yet if one of these savages has all the logical ground for his beliefs taken away, he doesn't stop believing. He then calls his mistaken beliefs "faith" because he knows they are right. And he knows they are right because he has faith. This is an unbreakable circle of false logic that can't be touched. In reality, it is plain mental inertia. A case of thinking "what always was" will also "always be". And not wanting to blast the thinking patterns out of the old rut.

'Mental inertia alone is not going to cause trouble – there is cultural inertia too. Some of you in this room believe my conclusions and would like to change. But will all your people change? The unthinking ones, the habit-ridden, reflex-formed people who *know* what is now will always be. They'll act like a drag on whatever plans you make, whatever attempts you undertake to progress with the new knowledge you have.'

'Then it's useless, there's no hope for our world?' Rhes asked.

'I didn't say that,' Jason answered. 'I merely mean that your troubles won't end by throwing some kind of mental switch. I see three courses open for the future, and the chances are that all three will be going on at the same time.

'First – and best – will be the rejoining of city and country Pyrrans into the single human group they came from. Each is incomplete now, and has something the other one needs. In the city here you have science and contact with the rest of the galaxy. You also have a deadly war. Out there in the jungle, your first cousins live at peace with the world, but lack medicine and the other benefits of scientific knowledge, as well as any kind of cultural contact with the rest of mankind. You'll both have to join together and benefit from the exchange. At the same time you'll have to forget the superstitious hatred you have of each other. This will only be done outside of the city, away from the war. Every one of you who is capable should go out voluntarily, bringing some fraction of the knowledge that needs sharing. You won't be harmed if you go in good faith. And you will learn how to live *with* this planet, rather than against it. Eventually you'll have civilized communities that won't be either "grubber" or "junkman". They'll be Pyrran.'

'But what about our city here?' Kerk asked.

'It'll stay right here – and probably won't change in the slightest. In the beginning you'll need your perimeter and defences to stay alive, while the people are leaving. And after that it will keep going because there are going to be any number of people here who you won't convince. They'll stay and fight and eventually die. Perhaps you will be able to do a better job in educating their children. What the eventual end of the city will be, I have no idea.'

They were silent as they thought about the future. On the floor, Skop groaned but did not move. 'Those are two ways,' Meta said. 'What is the third?'

'The third possibility is my own pet scheme,' Jason smiled. 'And I hope I can find enough people to go along with me. I'm going to take my money and spend it all on outfitting the best and most modern spacer, with every weapon and piece of scientific equipment I can get my hands on. Then I'm going to ask for Pyrran volunteers to go with me.'

'What in the world for?' Meta frowned.

'Not for charity. I expect to make my investment back, and more. You see, after these past few months, I can't possibly return to my old occupation. Not only do I have enough money now to make it a waste of time, but I think it would be an unending bore. One thing about Pyrrus – if you live – is that it spoils you for the quieter places. So I'd like to take this ship that I mentioned and go into the business of opening up new worlds. There are thousands of planets where men would like to settle, only getting a foothold on them is too rough or rugged for the usual settlers. Now can you imagine a planet a Pyrran couldn't lick after the training you've had here? And wouldn't you enjoy doing it?'

'There would be more than pleasure involved, though. In the city your lives have been geared for continual deadly warfare. Now you're faced with the choice of a fairly peaceful future, or staying in the city to fight an unnecessary and foolish war. I offer the third alternative of the occupation you know best, that would let you accomplish something constructive at the same time.

'Those are the choices. Whatever wou decide is up to each of you personally.'

Before anyone could answer, livid pain circled Jason's throat. Skop had regained consciousness and surged up from the floor. He pulled Jason from the chair with a single motion, holding him by the neck, throttling him. The bowmen tried to shoot, but held their fire because Jason was in the way.

'Kerk! Meta!' Skop shouted hoarsely. 'Grab guns! Open the locks – our people'll be here, kill the damn grubbers and their lies!'

Jason tore at the fingers that were choking the life out of him, but it was like pulling at bent steel bars. He couldn't talk and the blood hammered in his ears and drowned his thoughts. It was over now and he had lost. They'd butcher each other in the spaceship and Pyrrus would keep on being a deathworld until every one of them was dead.

Meta hurtled forward like an uncoiled spring and the crossbows twanged. One bolt caught her in the leg, the other transfixed her upper arm. But she had been shot as she jumped and her inertia carried her across the room, to her fellow Pyrran and the dying off-worlder.

She raised her good arm and chopped down with the edge of her hand.

It caught Skop a hard blow on the biceps and his arm jumped spasmodically, his hand leaping from Jason's throat.

'What are you doing?' he shouted in strange terror to the wounded girl who fell against him. He pushed her away, still clutching Jason with his other hand. She didn't answer. Instead she chopped again, hard and true, the edge of her hand catching Skop across the windpipe, crushing it. He dropped Jason and fell to the floor, retching and gasping.

Jason watched the end through a haze, barely conscious.

Skop struggled to his feet, turned pain-filled eyes to his friends. 'You're wrong,' Kerk said. 'Don't do it!'

The sound the wounded man made was more animal than human. When he dived towards the guns on the far side of the room, the crossbows twanged like harps of death. He skidded into the guns, his hand knocking them aside, but he was already dead.

When Brucco went over to help Meta, no one interfered. Jason gasped air back into his lungs, breathing in life. The watching glass eye of the viewer carried the scene to everyone in the city.

'Thanks, Meta . . . for understanding . . . as well as helping.' Jason had to force the words out.

'Skop was wrong and you were right, Jason,' she said. Her voice broke for a second as Brucco snapped off the feathered end of the steel bolt with his fingers, and pulled the shaft out of her arm. 'I can't stay in the city; only people who feel as Skop did will be able to do that. And I'm afraid I can't go into the forest – you saw what luck I had with the stingwing. If it's all right, I'd like to come with you. I'd like to very much.'

It hurt when he talked, so Jason could only smile, but she knew what he meant.

Kerk looked down in unhappiness at the body of the dead man. 'He was wrong – but I know how he felt. I can't leave the city, not yet. Someone will have to keep things in hand while the changes are taking place. Your ship is a good idea, Jason, you'll have no shortage of volunteers. Though I doubt if you'll get Brucco to go with you.'

'Of course not,' Brucco snapped, not looking up from the compression bandage he was tying. 'There's enough to do right here on Pyrrus. The animal life, quite a study to be made, probably have every ecologist in the galaxy visiting here before long. But I'll be first.'

Kerk walked slowly to the screen overlooking the city. No one attempted to stop him. He looked out at the buildings, the smoke still curling up from the perimeter, and the limitless sweep of green jungle beyond.

'You've changed it all, Jason,' he said. 'We can't see it now, but Pyrrus will never be the way it was before you came. For better or worse.'

'Better, damn it, better,' Jason croaked, and rubbed his aching throat. 'Now get together and end this war, so that people will really believe it.'

Rhes turned and, after an instant's hesitation, extended his hand to Kerk. The grey-haired Pyrran felt the same repugnance himself about touching a grubber, the memory of a lifetime of disgust.

But they shook hands then because they were both strong men.

MILLENNIUM

JOHN VARLEY

JUST WHEN YOU THOUGHT IT WAS SAFE TO GO BACK INTO THE FUTURE...

Someone fouls up and leaves a twonky behind. A twonky's the kind of thing that, for the surreptitious time-traveller, can really spell disaster. In this case, it was Pinky's stunner – a 99th-century weapon mislaid on a 20th-century airliner.

And what were Pinky and the snatch squad doing there anyway? Believe it or not, rescuing the victims of an about-to-be-fatal accident, transporting them safely into the future and putting dummies in their place. Because there's no point in tinkering with the timestream, and people will expect to find bodies in a plane crash.

But not twonkies. So someone had to stay there and look for the damn thing, because if anyone ever found out, the whole future could be finished long before it ever begun...

'Brilliant, inventive and satisfying.'

New York Times Book Review

GENERAL FICTION   0 7221 8839 0   £1.99

**In a future world of strangers,
the hunter and the hunted are one . . .**

ROGER ZELAZNY

Winner of 3 Nebula and 3 Hugo Awards

William Blackhorse Singer, the last Navajo tracker on a future
earth, has stocked the Interstellar Life Institute with its most
exotic creatures. But one of Singer's prizes preys upon his
mind: a metamorph. The one-eyed shapeshifter Cat, whose
home planet has been destroyed. Singer offers Cat freedom to
help him defend Earth against a terrible predator, and Cat
accepts. The price: permission to hunt the hunter. And the
deadly game begins. In a fierce, global hunt, Singer flees his
extra-sentient killer. And suddenly, he is pursuing not life, but
the mysteries of his people, and the blinding vision of his own
primeval spirit . . .

'Zelazny's best book since *Lord of Light*.' *Joe Haldeman*.
'The interweaving of old tales and futuristic adventures is
genuinely moving . . .'
New York Times Book Review.
'The melting together of perceptions of the future and the past
are brilliant, effective and moving.'
Vonda McIntyre.

SCIENCE FICTION   0 7221 9442 0   **£1.95**

Also available by Roger Zelazny in Sphere Science Fiction:

THE HAND OF OBERON   NINE PRINCES IN AMBER
MY NAME IS LEGION   THE GUNS OF AVALON
SIGN OF THE UNICORN   THE COURTS OF CHAOS
DAMNATION ALLEY

A selection of bestsellers from SPHERE

FICTION

DELCORSO'S GALLERY	Philip Caputo	£2.25 ☐
SOPHIE	Judith Saxton	£1.95 ☐
THE BRITISH CROSS	Bill Granger	£1.95 ☐
COMPANY SECRETS	Andrew Coburn	£2.25 ☐
FALL RIVER LINE	Daoma Winston	£2.95 ☐

FILM & TV TIE-INS

THE RIVER	Steven Bauer	£1.95 ☐
WATER	Gordon McGill	£1.75 ☐
THE LEGEND OF THE DOOZER		
WHO DIDN'T	Louise Gikow	£1.50 ☐
BEST FRIENDS	Jocelyn Stevenson	£1.50 ☐
NO-ONE KNOWS WHERE GOBO GOES		
	Mark Saltzman	£1.50 ☐

NON-FICTION

INTREPID'S LAST CASE	William Stevenson	£2.25 ☐
TALKING TO MYSELF	Anna Raeburn	£1.95 ☐
AROUND THE WORLD IN 78 DAYS		
	Nicholas Coleridge	£1.95 ☐
HAVING A BABY	Danielle Steel and others	£3.95 ☐
A JOBBING ACTOR	John Le Mesurier	£1.95 ☐

All Sphere books are available at your local bookshop or newsagent, or can be ordered direct from the publisher. Just tick the titles you want and fill in the form below.

Name _____

Address _____

_____

Write to Sphere Books, Cash Sales Department, P.O. Box 11, Falmouth, Cornwall TR10 9EN

Please enclose cheque or postal order to the value of the cover price plus:

UK: 55p for the first book, 22p for the second book and 14p for each additional book ordered to a maximum charge of £1.75.

OVERSEAS: £1.00 for the first book plus 25p per copy for each additional book.

BFPO & EIRE: 55p for the first book, 22p for the second book plus 14p per copy for the next 7 books, thereafter 8p per book.

Sphere Books reserve the right to show new retail prices on covers which may differ from those previously advertised in the text or elsewhere, and to increase postal rates in accordance with the PO.